The Pugville Chronicles

Volume One

Making It Home

Michael Dean Jacobs and Kevin E. Thompson

ISBN:9781797768304

Written by Michael Dean Jacobs
Story by Kevin E. Thompson and Michael Dean Jacobs
Illustrations by Foreshadow Films, ForeshadowFilms.com
Additional art by Matthew Keranen, Heavy-Ordnance.com
Edited by William Greenleaf, GreenleafLiteraryServices.com

Registration pending.

Table of Contents

This book is dedicated to the pugs of Juniper Avenue who made every place a home, and who waited patiently by Dad's favorite chair to tell of their great adventures.

May they live forever in the imaginations of those they loved the best: family, friends, and friends with bacon. We humbly take credit for their work.

CHAPTER ONE

Lost

Snuffy bellyflopped in the mud and flexed his claws to stop sliding. He cursed loudly at the stinging rain. He cursed himself for not escaping its monumental destruction. He had a sick feeling in his gut for wanting to leave Tinkerbelle behind if she couldn't keep up.

"Stop looking for him!" he shouted. "He wouldn't slow down to look for you."

"He's your brother, for God's sake!" she cried through the blinding wind. "We can't leave him here."

"Yes, he is my brother," Snuffy responded, "and you should be glad he isn't yours and come on."

As he carried on up the hill, Tinkerbelle stood firm with a terrible look of disdain. There wasn't time for this. The neighborhood was falling apart, and the only way to safety was up a treacherous hill. If Tuffy wasn't already ahead of them, going back toward the floods and wreckage would be suicide.

"Look," Snuffy said, "we both know he acts differently around you, but he'll never leave this place. He'll only try to make us all stay. He's got a screw loose. He thinks he should be people. He has spent his stinking life proving how smart he is—and I hope he's right. But I'm taking my pug butt away from here before we're all dead. You want to stay, suit yourself."

Snuffy had argued for weeks that it was time to go, time to stay ahead of the carnage that was now overwhelming them. They were family dogs with no family left, so it was time to find their purpose elsewhere. But his big brother always knew better. If Snuffy ever found a bacon tree, Tuffy would find a reason not to climb it.

Tinkerbelle was a calming influence in the brothers' lives. When she joined their home, the family just worked better. But these relentless storms had changed everything in a way that could never be normal again. They all instinctively knew that Mother Nature was choosing them over people, that this was a cosmic shift in the food chain. They all knew that being pugs made them different from other dogs, that pugs were leaders and champions. Tuffy understood that better than anyone.

But Snuffy the family dog, who'd been adopted into a loving home to care for wonderful children, knew none of it mattered if you didn't survive. He saw the old neighborhood as a war zone. The pounding rains were like artillery fire, the wreckage like bombed-out ruins, and no sign of people except the tonnage of personal effects that continued to spill from the broken homes. He meant to survive this war.

Snuffy had never been up the steep hill they were climbing. He focused on one foothold at a time through the sludge. He looked back to see the houses collapsing and belongings rushing in rivers of waste. His stomach jumped in fear, giving him the extra traction he needed to make it up the muddy slope.

Finally at the crest of the hill, he saw a sprawling flat land scattered with manicured ranches, all neatly cut into groves of bountiful trees. He took it all in for the tiniest moment, raised his eyebrows in a look of possible good fortune, and shouted the encouraging report to Tinkerbelle. She made the crest, and they broke into a trot across the soaked grass.

Snuffy stopped deep in a clump of trees. The thick branches overhead gave welcome relief from the cold rain, and they could once again sniff around. Wind to a dog is like darkness. Snuffy shook his coat and gave Tinkerbelle a nuzzle, realizing at once his fear for his brother's safety and his gratitude for her company.

For the moment, they were safe. Wherever they were, it wasn't falling apart, and that was good enough. He joined Tinkerbelle, scratching and biting some fluffy vegetation hanging low to the ground. Soon they were curled together, resting.

Snuffy dreamed vividly about his big brother. They were in the backyard of the family home on a beautiful sunny day. Tuffy was showing off for Tinkerbelle, and they were all laughing. Tuffy predictably took it too far. He started playing too rough, banging his little brother around for real, and the laughing turned to alarm and reprimands. Tuffy turned mean, the way he did when he was wrong and wouldn't admit it, and began belittling Snuffy and really hurting him. Snuffy grew frightened and angry.

In the dream, he watched himself advance a furious scowl straight at his brother's flat face. His black eyes glowed with rage, his tubby body swelled with muscles, and his short legs extended in height. He grew taller and rounder to match his anger until he was a giant pug towering over a tiny, frightened bully with nowhere to run. He watched his giant self stomp and feint attacks toward his punk brother just for a laugh as his dream body grew into the sky. He was towering over the neighborhood and could see the whole place at once. Tuffy was like a bug that he could crush effortlessly.

Then a sudden paralyzing chill coursed through his gargantuan body, and he knew he'd grown too tall. He panicked, wanting to shrink back to earth, back to warmth.

He woke feeling the brutal cold of his dream. It took a moment to realize that the numbing water of a turgid flood had overtaken their refuge, and he and Tinkerbelle were surfing their leafy bed fast into darkness. The wind was freezing, and rain was falling like rocks.

Tinkerbelle snapped awake and capsized them into the gushing current. Snuffy dunked under, moving fast. As soon as he surfaced, the floating barge of a giant tree limb pushed him under again. He clawed a tight grip on the underside, and with all his might he kicked and grappled to the top. The faint cry of Tinkerbelle's gurgling voice came from the trailing branches that were keeping this log buoyant, and she clawed her way beside Snuffy. They clung tightly to one another atop the titanic log, ferrying off into nothingness.

JACSON AV

Tuffy growled and snarled his meanest face at the dripping and mortified rat, who scurried up the nearest tree. "That's right." Tuffy laughed maniacally. "Up the tree you go." Tuffy gave a nod to Snake, his new friend unhoused by the waters. "Can you do it?"

Tuffy smiled as the viper wound his way up the tree trunk, then scuttled sideways to catch the rat like a centerfielder under a fly ball. "See?" he declared. "isn't this more fun than eating the little fella?"

Tuffy hadn't given a second thought to the well-being of his brother or Tinkerbelle. He hadn't given the first thought about the danger these storms foreboded, and made no effort to secure anything but a good time. He just enjoyed the afternoon in what they called the jungle, a neighborhood park surrounded by thick shrubbery, high at the edge of the farthest hill.

Tuffy let the rat hit the ground. He gave him a head start before giving chase.

The rat stopped suddenly and turned to face his tormentors. "That's it!" he exclaimed. "You want to eat me? Eat me. I can't escape you, so go ahead. I hope I have rabies."

Tuffy was sincerely shocked at the rat's perception of his little game. "Whoa, little fella," he said. "Nobody's going to hurt you. We're including you. You're one of the boys."

Tuffy considered himself an expert in the habits of successful people, and this humiliation was a friendly game he'd seen a hundred times before. Tuffy held out great people as heroes. He also knew how people were weak. All he ever wanted was to perfect the world where common people had failed. Playing out a power dynamic with his new friends was as natural as scratching his own butt.

"Are you nuts?" The rat was hyperventilating. "Your snake friend wants to eat me, and you're bouncing me off the ground. This is a game you play with friends?"

"It's what people do," Tuffy said. "I like to do what people do." He knew it was time to express generosity to those lesser than himself. "You stick with us and everything's going to be all right," he said condescendingly. "Like we were really going to eat you."

Tuffy and his new pals climbed to a high point in the jungle, looking for a different game. Tuffy marveled at how broken and displaced everything was—all the stuff that people had held dear. He spotted couches and tables loose and abandoned. A pug could climb on a couch all he wanted in this scenario. He saw gold and gems sparkling in the rushing waters, and remembered how these things had brought people status and envy. He saw a world of treasure abandoned and unprotected, and he began to think that he was meant to inherit it all.

The trio scoped out the jungle for the safest, highest ground.

Then Tuffy turned toward his friends and smiled. "Let's talk about how we're going to rule the world."

Snuffy couldn't be sure how many hours passed before the gray light of dawn revealed a small stretch of high ground. Desperate and weary, they kicked and paddled for it. Snuffy allowed himself to hope the worst was over as the storm momentarily calmed. He wept for joy over solid earth. The sun peeked through, and Snuffy stretched his neck to soak in all the warmth he could.

His nostrils flared, and his belly ached at the smell of something sweet. "Food," he mumbled, his eyes still closed. "I can smell food."

He hit all fours and sniffed wildly around every shrub and branch. Tinkerbelle did the same in the opposite direction. Snuffy lapped up a sweet berry from the ground and yelped in delight. Tinkerbelle shot to his side, and they devoured a branchful of colorful fruit.

The sky darkened, and ominous thunder clapped in the distance. Snuffy followed a trail of minty leaves and sweet berries toward a nearby rock formation. It led like bread crumbs to a small cave. The rain began again as the two pugs sniffed carefully ever closer to shelter.

When they finally peeked their heads inside, a giant bear leaped from the shadows with a ferocious roar. The pugs retreated in panic. They ran back toward the water, which was fast swallowing the small patch of land. The gigantic bear loosed another fearsome growl and caught up in an instant. The dogs were trapped between the icy water and the murderous brute. They rolled themselves into a single ball of pug and braced for the attack.

"I'm sorry," Snuffy whispered in Tink's ear, "I was never really mad at you. I'm so sorry . . ."

"Shhh," Tinkerbelle murmured, burying her nose deep into Snuffy's fur. "None of that matters now. Try to be still."

"You're my best friend," Snuffy said, barely breathing. "I just want you to know you're my best friend . . ."

A monumental thunderclap sounded directly overhead. Blistering rain fell again as if from buckets, and biting winds blew anew. The dogs lay as still as possible with their eyes shut tightly. The ground shook beneath them as the bear rose and stomped a furious racket.

And then the bear stopped. He looked closely at the two pugs, clinging to one another because they were all they had left. The exhibition calmed the ferocious beast, and he transformed. Literally. He lowered his stance and bowed his head. He retracted his claws. And then something magical happened.

His back rounded and transformed into a hard shell. His furry, powerful arms retracted into the shell and returned as scaly turtle legs. His massive head slid into the shell as a frightening bear and out again as a kindly terrapin.

Snuffy opened one eye and then the other, clearly not being devoured. He couldn't believe the bear was gone.

"This water ain't getting any lower," said the turtle, lowering his hind part into the wet sand. "Best you both climb on my back so we stand a chance of getting out of here."

And so they climbed aboard the magical creature, and into the wet darkness they rode. Day turned to night, and then again into day. It was impossible to know how many times.

They finally landed on the shore of a beautiful, rich, green island. The sun was warm and bright.

CHAPTER TWO

Back Home

Tuffy was alive, and he felt exuberant. The claim he'd staked high in the jungle had kept them safe from destruction. Snake and Rat were fine. They were a team, forged not by fire but by rain, to the fulfillment of Tuffy's vision. They triumphantly navigated the soggy jungle to the spoils of good fortune.

The neighborhood was shambles. Just as Tuffy had predicted, the bathrooms and bedrooms and dens of the neighborhood—and everything within them—were spilled into the streets. Tuffy beamed with delight as he took personal credit for all of it. They dug through muddy pockets of delicacies washed out of the neighborhood kitchens and scrounged their bellies full. Tuffy's new world was sloppy with riches of junk and people treasure. Every mudhole and withering stream held the makings of Tuffy's dream life. Realizing he couldn't keep what he couldn't carry, Tuffy formally declared their priority a suitable base of operations.

Most houses were in random states of collapse, and the best part, were overflowing with riches. Tuffy picked a mostly upright split-level as good enough and pushed easily through the front door. It slowly dawned on him that he was in the very house he'd abandoned so many days earlier, his old family home. He searched in vain for the slim possibility he'd find his brother and the girl while giving his new partners a tour.

The kitchen cabinets remained in place, and Rat gleefully climbed the shelves, trying to decipher labels. Tuffy nosed through the pantry door and was cracked head over tail by the door shoving back from the inside. Tuffy swung his mighty rear into the panel and burst the door wide open. He heard a shriek and then a crash. The three looked inside to find a furry mole splayed akimbo against the bottom shelf, all manner of boxes and cans cascading around him. The mole tried to speak, then collapsed in a heap. Minutes later, Mole was the newest member of the team.

Tuffy assembled his new crew like family at the kitchen table, passing and slopping down all the food they could break out of random packages. Tuffy expounded his philosophy of provider, the manner by which the father figure is rewarded with wealth and station and authority.

"I lived with people," he explained, "they were diabolical and civilized at the same time."

The world was like a pyramid to Tuffy, the higher you sat, the better your life. "People failed who fostered independence. There has to be order or people get hurt." Tuffy explained how everything was now theirs if only they would take it.

Tuffy had Mole immediately onboard. He confirmed the value of work and the pride of caring for one's own. Tuffy let Rat know there was a place and a purpose for him, and Rat was happy just to be alive and not hungry.

Snake listened suspiciously. It wasn't his nature to join groups and work toward common goals. "I don't join things," he said, "I'll hang around, but if you're hustling me..." He didn't finish the thought. He simply uncoiled himself in a flash, snapping Rat off the table, threatening to swallow him in front of the group.

"Enough. Stop." Tuffy made calming gestures, "I understand. Join us or don't...but please drop the rat."

Snake took a long mean stare at the pug and then spit the rodent to the floor. The rat gathered himself while mumbling filthy admonitions under his breath.

Walking the street with a well-fed crew was intoxicating for Tuffy. He, Mole, and Rat walked abreast down the ruins of what had been a provincial haven, and Tuffy was lord of all he surveyed.

Snake kept to the margins, slithering in and out of sight, the perfect wingman. Tuffy wished his little brother and the girl would show up and see him now.

Tuffy stopped them at times to root through broken shelves and caches of goods. He directed Mole and Rat to fashion a sled from the wreckage and drag along all manner of trophies and staples. Rat immediately tired of the chore.

Back in the jungle, Tuffy ordered the crew to take the goods to the house. Snake was already slithered deep in the brush, and Tuffy was bathed in a great sense of purpose as he followed. He knew that he was destined for great things.

As he approached the shoreline, he saw Snake stalking a group of tasty-looking ducks just inside the water. Snake was slithering silently on a wide path around the birds, trying to isolate one to attack. The very small crackle of Tuffy's footstep caused the birds to scatter and land again in the lake many yards away. Snake shot him a filthy look as Tuffy froze in his tracks. They approached the water together, watching the ducks paddle and quack. At the water's edge, still not convinced they were completely without a chance at the fowl, they stood in silence.

Suddenly they were splashed with cold water and blinded by the gaping maw of a giant alligator's mouth. It snapped down inches from them. Tuffy leaped three feet backward, landing on his head, and continued to tumble. Snake slithered leeward as fast as a shadow and up the nearest tree. The monster slowly unmucked from the perfect hiding spot and made land. Tuffy stared at him, petrified.

"Darn it, you guys," the huge beast said in a soft and soothing voice. "Duck is maybe the most delicious thing ever . . ." He shook the mud from his feet as he walked straight toward Tuffy. He was easily tall enough to reach the top of the slide in the sandpit where the children played. He had scales like armor, and two fat teeth hung like shiny baseball bats on either side of his dinosaur mouth. "Didja ever have duck?"

Tuffy, eyes like saucers, still trying to breathe, managed a weak, "N-n-n-no."

"Aww, you're missing out. You really are." The mammoth reptile stepped so close that he gave Tuffy a fraternal poke on the shoulder. His arms were so short they didn't seem to belong on this reptilian nightmare. "Hey, they're still out there. Heck, they're everywhere. Wanna catch a few with me?"

Snake made ground and approached the two at a wide berth. All they could see was the tall grass bending in zigs and zags until he popped his head out of the weeds. Tuffy started to breathe again.

"The name's Crock," the dinosaur reported with a gentle nod.

"Hi, Crock," Tuffy said, tilting his head to the side dog-style. "Aren't you an alligator?"

"Who can tell?" Crock asked, leaning in frighteningly close. "Last time I heard my own name, it was Crock. I been living in the pipes for years. Jeez, I'm hungry."

"So you lived in the sewers?" Tuffy asked carefully.

"Yeah. They go all under the place. I'd come out sometimes when the pipes landed at a field or at a water somewhere . . . catch a few ducks. Ducks! Ohhhh, ducks."

"And you're still hungry?"

"Real hungry."

Tuffy studied the enormity of the beast and knew right away how Crock fit into his plan. "Come with us," he said, and they all walked away.

Rat nearly fainted at the sight of the pre-historic monster coming into view from the kitchen window. He scrambled to hide in the pantry behind a bargain-sized can of tuna.

Tuffy made a place for the behemoth, and called out for Rat's assistance. Getting no answer, Tuffy stomped to the pantry and scanned the shelves.

"You say you like duck?" Tuffy asked. "This here'll suit you very well."

Tuffy grabbed the tuna can and revealed Rat, the shivering runaway. He shot him a deadly stare while he asked, "How do your people like the taste of rats?"

"Rats are good. Got to find a lot of 'em," Crock opined. Tuffy raised a sinister brow.

"Tuna fish, is it?" Rat was now talking fast and moving faster, " Lemme get that for you boss, we'll have this open in a jif we will, that's what we'll do, open this can right up and serve it to you and your friends..."

Tuffy stifled his displeasure and returned to the table.

Somehow the can was pried open and managed across the room.

Crock eyeballed Rat as if to say he wasn't enough to eat, and then caught the pungent whiff of seafood. Crock took can and all and began masticating the entire arrangement. Tuffy offered Rat a gracious pat on the head to indicate he was friend and not food, and Rat bowed and scraped his way out of there.

Tuffy cajoled and connived to get every survivor on board with his plan to turn the old neighborhood into a model factory town. All the ruins would be pillaged, all the inhabitable spaces restored. The resources would pay for service to his empire. He gave Mole his own crews for scavenging, and Snake a crew of slumdogs and vipers for intimidation and security. He made Crock his personal bodyguard and Rat his lackey and valet. Tuffy was provider and protector, the magnanimous source of a good life for all. Tuffy was living his dream, doing what people do.

Next, Tuffy saved the life of a frightened cockroach and graciously offered him a reconditioning concession. Roach had ants cleaning and carrying, termites sanding and painting, and cockroaches filling cabinets with food and other necessities. It was an amazing feat of engineering. And everyone was indebted to the head pug in charge. They worked to Tuffy's benefit and paid Tuffy for rent and supplies. Just like people do.

Tuffy dedicated himself to returning his family to a perfected version of their old home. He remembered how people invited guests to covet the opulence of one's home and possessions. Tuffy crafted a specific guest list for such an event, and meticulously prepared the main house with his most impressive possessions on display. The mole crew ransacked the collection for the most delicious foods. Housewares were sifted for the most opulent settings. Crock, Snake, and a collection of enforcers would be on hand to intimidate, and Rat would be at Tuffy's beck and call to impress. The event would celebrate Tuffy's wealth and authority posing as an act of openness and generosity.

Tuffy graciously mingled as he had seen mingling at people gatherings, regaling all with a funny or touching tale of life among people. Tuffy embellished each story to remember himself as the central figure, telling of times he did this for people and how they would count on him for that. He told also of people's inhumanity. He made a fine case for how these were fortunate times, the kind and generous days.

Tuffy gifted some trinkets to the most impressionable, intending them to spread the gospel of his magnanimity. He knew that to take copiously one had to share generously. Tuffy always exchanged kindness for loyalty. Just like people do.

CHAPTER THREE

Pugville

Snuffy awoke to the familiar smell of the only meal he'd had in days. The magical sea turtle had foraged a breakfast feast from the nearby shrubbery.

"Thanks," Snuffy and Tinkerbelle said as they gobbled the food gratefully.

"I'm more than happy to be of service," Bertrand said.

"Can you help us find our way home?" Snuffy asked.

"I don't have a clue. I don't even know where we are. But I have an idea of how to find things." The old turtle was a scientist of sorts, and he explained how he'd developed a system of charting and measuring unfamiliar places. Bertrand shared how he always tried to visit new places, to learn about their similarities and differences.

"I've always felt that way about people," Snuffy said.

The beach they were on looked very much the same in each direction, so they decided to explore away from the water.

Bertrand rummaged a fat stick from the nearby berm and tied a long green leaf to it, then Snuffy helped him pound it into the sand at their feet. This, Snuffy learned, would be the first guidepost for discovering all the rest.

A short climb across the thick berm exposed a glorious valley. Tinkerbelle nearly swooned over the beauty as she called out every feature. There were thickets of trees and open meadows. There were flowers of all colors and sizes. And there was the narrowest of crystal blue streams running down the inland mountain into a shimmering lake. The berm climbed and circled in both directions, and the stream disappeared into a dense forest.

Snuffy thought he might see the way home from the high side, so the three of them walked the perimeter, planting more flags at pertinent points. Bertrand was excellent at spotting food and natural resources, and he reveled in description and explanation as he marked them.

As they continued on, they heard a faint cry for help from a wide patch of ivy. Snuffy laid his nose to the ground and jogged straight to a momma pig, enormous with child, moaning in quiet agony.

"This child is coming, and he's coming now," she whispered. "I can't do this."

Immediately understanding the severity of the situation, Snuffy reared his head and loosed a great howl of distress. Then he stood helpless while Bertrand collected some therapeutic leaves and roots, then smashed a soothing compress together for the mother's forehead. Minutes passed and Snuffy sent another howl skyward.

"My goodness, what a howl. Are you in pain? What's the big emergency to cause such a howling?" The voice came from a beautiful brown bear who leaned in among the startled group. "Oh, I see," the bear said, noticing the pig. "Well, step aside, all of you. I suppose I'm the only one who's ever seen a birthing?"

"I guess," Snuffy replied.

"No time for guessing," the bear said. "We're having a baby. Go on, step aside." She pushed her way beside the momma pig.

Snuffy was overwhelmed by the scene. It was gory and obviously painful, and he felt helpless. Wanting to turn and run made him feel guilty, but watching made him feel sick.

Bertrand dug right in with his roots and leaves. Seeing the momma competently attended provided some relief. Still, Snuffy and Tinkerbelle paced like expectant grandparents as time ticked on, and on. The cross talk between the attendants grew alarming. The baby wasn't coming, and the mother wasn't well. They used her name, shouting encouragement to hang on and to talk to them. The bear yanked and pulled at the baby, and Bertrand massaged and manipulated the momma. By the time the baby was born, his momma was unconscious.

The brown bear laid the piglet in the soft ivy, and he began to feed. He looked like a monster next to his mother. She was in every way an ordinary pig, but he looked like a wild boar, with a giant head and a long, pronounced snout. Bertrand and the bear walked the short distance to the running stream while the pugs sat and watched the new family.

The group made camp in the ivy on the side of the hill. They managed a fire, and they gathered a fine meal from the fertile land. Bertrand, being secretly a bear himself, was busy chatting with Sarah, the midwife bear. They spoke of understanding nature and all she provides. Their connection made the old man feel a little flushed.

Mercy, the momma pig, was sleeping soundly with her son at her side. She had regained consciousness earlier, but she was weak. There was nothing they could do but watch her.

Snuffy was feeling better about the whole arrangement—the baby was born, Mercy was alive, and they all had full bellies. He felt calm and safe for the first time in recent memory. He had great respect for his new friends, and he'd been lost in worse places.

Many other survivors had made camps on the shore of the lake, and the nighttime glowed with fires twinkling in the water's reflection. Snuffy watched and wondered how every story compared to his own. There still were no people. They'd vanished, as if the brutal storms were nature's way of washing them off the planet.

Snuffy and Tinkerbelle spent the next morning meeting the groups along the lake. Snuffy met a squirrel couple, Sammy and Sylvia. They were stockpiling supplies in hopes of finding the rest of their extended family. Snuffy paired them with Bertrand to make a food pantry.

Snuffy spread the word that everyone in the valley was welcome to take if they needed. "It's what people do," he said.

Moe the mule and his sons could drag logs and rocks to make shelter. Snuffy and Tinkerbelle told of communities of people working together and asked if there was a way to build common structures for the town.

He talked to everyone about pooling skills and supplies. Snuffy had no intention of staying in this place, but if living with people had taught him anything, it was that communities help each other. "It's what people do," he said again.

Moe and his sons thought to build a town square. They could clear land so resources could be gathered and supplies traded there. The squirrels had cousins and nephews and nieces who could do detail work and volunteered their services when they found their way out of the woods. Other neighbors felt themselves expert at finding food, and some considered themselves gourmet chefs. Snuffy encouraged and facilitated cooperation.

Sarah presented a wide collection of natural medicinal concoctions. She told how it all helps keep you well. "Nature is abundant with foods and cures," she said, offering a branch filled with antiseptic leaves for a whiff. "You just have to know where to look."

Snuffy walked the wide curve of the lake, away from the bustling neighbors. He searched the surrounding tree line for any clue to find a way home. He strained to see where the thin river topped the hill, certain there was a vista where he could see his brother digging around the muddy neighborhood. Tinkerbelle was soon at his side, gleefully evaluating the nesting opportunities of their rich new valley.

"Yes, I see it," he responded to Tinkerbelle's enthusiasm scornfully. "I see it all. But it's not for us."

"Of course it's for us. It's for all of us and it's wonderful," Tinkerbelle said.

"Not for us, Tink. We have to go home." Snuffy cast his gaze to the ground. He didn't have the courage for another dangerous journey, but in his gut he knew it was required. He had to find a way back home, with or without Tinkerbelle. He also knew he'd never make it alone.

They both stood quietly and let the tension hang in the air.

Without deciding anything, they finally spotted a very large bear with a very blond coat keeping to himself on the far side of the lake. It was clear their discussion was best continued another time, and Snuffy walked off to see him. He was bizarre and a little frightening, and Snuffy approached him carefully.

"Hello there. How you doing? Are you also lost in the flood?"

The bear explained that he'd been living in the woods alone for the longest time before the rains began. "I been by myself since my coat gone yeller," he said. "Hard to take a bear serious when he's bright yeller, I guess."

"I guess," was all Snuffy could think to say.

"My name's Buck. I didn't know if I was welcome."

"Everybody will be included," Snuffy said, indicating the many creatures camped along the water. "We're all going to make a town, just like people."

"Never lived in a town," Buck said sadly. "Don't know how I could be any help 'less you need rasslin.' I'm pretty good at rasslin.'" The thought brought a big smile to the yellow bear.

"I wouldn't doubt that for a minute," Snuffy said. "There might be some rasslin' if you were sheriff. Would you look after the town as sheriff?"

Buck raised himself to even more unbelievable proportion.

Snuffy had to lean back to see his face. "It's what people do," Snuffy said.

Buck the yellow-blond bear gleefully accepted.

The next day, Buck was walking the valley at his new job. Moe and the squirrels had flattened a rusty bottle cap to wear as a badge. Out by the tree line, the sheriff heard a high-pitched squeal for help. It was a beautiful peahen being run around a tree by a gang of weasels.

"Halt!" Buck shouted, but received no response. "Stop!" He tried again, in case the varmints didn't know what halt meant.

"We heard ya the first time," the lead weasel yelled back, standing upright and stroking his furry tail with his tiny claws.

This made the rest laugh loudly and start throwing nuts at Buck's head.

The bear could ignore many slights, but being beaned in the melon with nuts wasn't one of them. He bolted toward the gang and trapped one in his huge paws. Then he lifted the little squirt as if to eat him in one gulp. This caused the weasels to reassemble and beg forgiveness for their misunderstood little friend, whining and crying like . . . well, weasels.

Buck dropped the little brat and pointed to the bottle cap stuck to his chest fur. "I'm the law in these parts," he shouted as the weasels scrambled.

Pandora Peahen fell into the big lug's arms.

"Are you all right?" Buck asked as he tried to check the hen for injury.

Pandora burst her bright plume and fanned herself. "I am now," she replied sweetly.

Buck instantly began to sweat, and his words started to stammer. As they made their way back toward the town, they discussed the storms, his hair, and how nice everyone was to take in a freak of a bear like him and trust him with a good job.

"I've always been an outcast too," Pandora shared. "I've always been alone."

Buck found Snuffy near the town square and introduced the hen.

"We're gonna have a new town here, and you're welcome to join us," Snuffy said. "Just do whatever it is that you do."

Buck continued to show the lady around. She suggested that all their cooperation needed organization. A town should know births and deaths and homes and businesses. Pandora talked herself right into a job.

Now that they had a sheriff, a clerk, and a town square, the animals decided things weren't right without a mayor. Snuffy was voted in unanimously. He made a speech to all his new friends, referencing how his ancestors were bred for noble service. Pugs had served emperors and kings, and being mayor was just as big an honor.

"I'm proud that a group so diverse could be so connected," he said. "You're all pugs in my book. In fact, we should call this place Pugville, a place where all are welcome and nobody is left behind."

Snuffy built a sign. He and Tinkerbelle spent all day scouting the perfect location, and Snuffy vowed to update the sign whenever the count changed. It would become his most beloved official duty. The sign read, simply, as follows:

PUGVILLE

Population: 26

Mercy wasn't getting better. All the natural medicine in the valley wasn't helping. She was asleep more than she was awake and had precious little time to know her baby. She called him Artemis. After Artemis was walking and weaned, Mercy quietly passed.

Snuffy and Tinkerbelle took the boy in hand and walked to each camp and home to break the news and invite everyone to the patch of ivy on the hill for a final goodbye.

"This patch is as far as Mercy could make it after the storm," Snuffy told the assembly. "This is where we found her, terribly ill, where she brought her boy into the world, and where she will rest forever."

There was a plot arranged by the construction crews. The beavers planned it, the squirrels set the tools, and the mules dug up the ground.

"She got to see her son born healthy," Snuffy said. "All she wanted was for her baby to be safe and well—and he always will be because Tinkerbelle and I will raise this fine pug as our very own."

This news surprised no one. It was the most sensible and natural thing that could happen. Tinkerbelle and Snuffy and Artemis had been bonded since his birth.

"And now," Snuffy continued, "I have a sign to change."

CHAPTER FOUR

Diplomacy

Mole returned to the main house scraped and beaten. He'd been investigating scavengers working in the blocks ahead of his crew and was jumped. He was badly hurt and struggled to finish his report. "We was robbed," he choked out.

"What did they get?" Tuffy asked, eyeballing Mole carefully to ensure he wasn't faking the theft.

"I didn't get that far." Mole wheezed and coughed, causing him to double over in pain. "I snuck around back and got my tail beat."

"Hogs?" Snake raised up to eye level the way a snake can do. "Was it the hogs?"

Mole only nodded that it was.

Tuffy, Snake, and Crock met a large group of razorback hogs at the tree line atop the hill. They stopped at a safe distance to look conciliatory.

"Hello, neighbors," Tuffy began. "We thought we'd come up and introduce ourselves . . ."

"We know who you are," the youngest of the gang interrupted. "Whatchoo want coming up here?"

"We wanted you to know that we have plenty of food and shelter. If you needed anything, we just wanted to do the neighborly thing and offer."

The young tough stared daggers at Tuffy through dark eyes set deep on either side of his barrel of a snout. His chest heaved as he scraped the dirt and then spat at the space between them through his deadly ivory tusks.

An older male edged his way in front of the aggressive youngster. "Well, thanks for sayin' it, but we don't need nothing.

His stab at diplomacy was accompanied by a quiet murmur of agreement.

Tuffy nodded. "Do you mind if I ask if you work this land?"

The mood quickly grew tense. The mob slowly widened, and Tuffy knew he might be in for a fight. He tried to make eye contact with the elder who had spoken up, but he wouldn't return the gaze. The group spread even wider.

A young adult male with a look of disappointment on his face was standing back, trying not to engage. The gang spread to optimal attack positions.

"Clete!" the young hog called out. "Clay, Buster, knock it off." He stepped forward. "Come here, all of you."

The mob relaxed and fell back into tighter ranks. Clete, Clay, and Buster approached the young hog's side.

"Look, mister," the hog said to Tuffy, soft-spoken and humble. "My cousins can get a little rowdy and act like jerks sometimes, but we mean you no disrespect. We don't want no trouble. We live up here and you down there. As long as it stays that way, everything's all right." He shot a hard look at Buster, who agreed with the slightest nod while scuffing at the dirt.

"Do you speak for the group?" Tuffy prodded.

"We all speak, but, yes . . . , I speak now for the group. We're all kin, and this here is our land. You folks are our guests, and it's best if you remember that."

Tuffy didn't take the bait. "Tuffy. Call me Tuffy." He intended to disarm the mob with a show of congeniality.

"The name's Anarkey. Folks call me Key," the hog played along. "These here's my cousins Clete and Clay, and I guess you met Buster."

Buster's face seemed stuck in its dirty look. Clete and Clay nodded stoic acknowledgments.

Tuffy took the hog aside, and they walked together. He realized that the high perch where they stood was the only way Snuffy and Tinkerbelle could have possibly escaped with their lives. He would provide a way to watch for their return and keep an eye on these hogs at the same time. It was also a perfect vista to see the neighborhood all at once.

"Tell you what," Tuffy suggested. "I might have a job for you, if you'll do it."

"What kind of job?" Anarkey asked suspiciously.

Tuffy told Key to fashion an observation platform under the giant willow tree. He reasoned that both could use it to keep an eye on the town. Tuffy didn't want a war with this crew, so it was best to never admit knowing what they were doing to his neighborhood. "If you do this well, there will be more jobs," Tuffy told Key. "There's plenty of work around the neighborhood to keep your cousins fed."

Key held his suspicions. He knew it served him to keep the pug close, so he accepted with all the grace he could imitate.

Tuffy was immersed in the spoils of his new station. He had his scavengers and refinishers tailor him a wardrobe of fine haberdashery. He wore a smart pocket vest, from which he hung a proper gold watch, and a dandy gentleman's hat cocked elegantly to one side. He'd selected a broken baseball bat to be carved and polished into a foppish walking stick. The getup made him feel like a boss, even if it made him look like a dancing pony.

He liked to walk the neighborhood just to be a presence, like a cheap gangster. He graciously greeted everyone, always en route to the coastline in the jungle. Tuffy felt strong and capable at the jungle, it was where he discovered that pugs were natural warriors. Where he'd spent so many days hustling games of chase and besting all comers with his ninja instincts.

Tuffy studied the shoreline. He paced and measured the slowly receding water. He could see that the floodwaters that cut off the neighborhood from the rest of the world were ebbing, but at a leaden pace. He knew in his gut that his family was alive somewhere beyond the water.

Tuffy paced the white lines cast in the dirt as the water crawled away, trying to put a time value to the very slightly increasing real estate. Then his solitude was broken by a shrill exhortation.

"You there! Dog! Flat face! Pug dog!"

It took Tuffy a moment to spot the withered and bent duck waddling his way.

"You, stupid. Yes, I'm talking to you."

The oldest living waterfowl he'd ever seen was closing on the pug, slowly but loudly.

"You Chinese dog?"

Tuffy wasn't sure if it was even a question.

"Hey, stupid! You Chinese dog, right?"

"Uh-huh," he finally responded, still unsure what to make of this.

"Well, I'm Chinese duck. How you like them apples?" The old bird took a swipe at him with her tiny walking stick.

"Nice to meet you."

"Wrong. Not nice." Madame Duck continued poking at the pug with her tiny cane. "Don't like you, dog. Special pug dog. Why you in my neighborhood? What you want around here? Not welcome." The duck was poking at the ground, at Tuffy, at nothing at all.

Tuffy was amused, but the feeling was wearing thin. "Hey," he said, raising his voice slightly to try to take control of the crazy animal. "Calm down and tell me what it is you're talking about . . . please?"

Tuffy dragged a clean log over for the elderly mallard, and the pair sat. Madame Duck explained that she'd been land-bound for years, not able to fly any longer with her flock. She had generations of children and grandchildren about whom she rambled, trying Tuffy's patience. He managed to get her back on message, and truthfully, he liked the old duck's spunk. He could have eaten her ten times by then. But there she was, still railing against Tuffy's very existence.

"Ancient Chinese emperors loved pug dogs," she said. "They also loved ducks . . . to eat." She was growing agitated again. "Why duck? Why they don't eat dog? You sit on lap, we sit on plate. Terrible!"

"What does that have to do with me?" Tuffy was still trying to calm the old duck.

"You friend with alligator. You friend with snake. You lousy pug dog."

"So?"

"So snake eat my family. Alligator eat my family. You get out my place."

"Ahhh, I see." Tuffy finally understood the point of the crazy duck's yammering. He let it sink in while she went off on another stick-waving tirade. "Tell you what," he said. "Your family flies here often, to care for you?"

"All the time. Fly all over world, my family."

"Yes, they fly all over this part of the world, for sure, right?"

"Always," the duck replied as she stuck her cane in the mud authoritatively.

"Okay. You have your family look around past this water for other pug dogs like me, let me know if you find them, and I'll see to it that nobody ever bothers you again."

"I ask my family to find more disgusting pug dogs? You crazy, or what?"

"Do this for me, and your family will never worry about Snake or Crocks . . . or anybody around here again."

The old duck considered the idea while giving Tuffy a terrible stink-eye. After a long pause, she softened a little, then began to cry. She dropped her stick and laid an ancient wing on Tuffy's shoulder. "You would do that for me?"

"It would be my pleasure."

"Okay. Deal. You okay for pug dog, you know that?"

"Thank you. Now let me help you back to your nest."

Tuffy escorted the bent animal to the brush, and then she chased him away, waving wildly with her stick. He returned to the water's edge and began to study more carefully the markings of the shoreline.

CHAPTER FIVE

Family

Snuffy's focus was split between his duties to this new place and his desperate desire to find his way home. His guiding principle was to be helpful and accepting, but the job of mayor was wearing him thin. He received townsfolk all day in his office and moderated all manner of problems and complaints.

The squirrels and the badgers were at odds over the burden of moving water from the lake to the town. The squirrels insisted that Snuffy approve an irrigation system. He listened to the squirrels argue in favor of trenches, which could be easily dug to bring freshwater close and relieve the backbreaking labor of carrying water like a prehistoric village. Snuffy thoroughly agreed with this position.

Then he sat with badgers, who argued that water was to be stopped and pooled, and never made to run, as it was unnatural and against nature. It would destroy the beauty of the place, they argued. They didn't want to live in a place with such blatant disregard for nature. Snuffy thoroughly agreed with this position as well.

Moe and Bertrand thought the canals were an excellent plan, both for the modern resource and the benefit of industry and purpose to their friends and neighbors. Snuffy thoroughly agreed with their positions too—and he couldn't wait until someone else was mayor.

Snuffy decided to put it to a vote and polled every single resident himself. He thought it only fair. It made him think of his brother. Tuffy would have barely listened, and then chose what he wanted anyway. Snuffy hated himself for wanting to be more like his brother.

Snuffy counted and recounted the votes. He had Pandora check his work. He even held the results for a day for those who might change their minds. It was decided that Pugville would have a freshwater system.

Bertrand was best qualified to oversee such a project, and the whole town agreed. He made a complicated office hung with maps and lists of measurements, routes, and impediments. Bertrand tapped Artemis as his apprentice, to learn the complex system at his knee. Artie was honored, but deep in his heart, he feared the assignment would make him seem different. Artemis was keenly aware that he was the only hog in Pugville, living in a family of pugs.

Artie had grown into a fine young boar, and Bertrand was very much a part of his family. Bertrand was like that special uncle who isn't really your uncle, a grown-up around whom you can be completely honest.

One day Artie was in a foul mood. He was brooding and stomping in an obvious way in front of Bertrand. His adoptive mother was having pups of her own, likely that afternoon, and Artie was expected to be home with them. "Do you think there'll be room for me once my mom has real kids?" he asked nervously.

"However could a kid be more real than you?" Bertrand gave him the slow, cocked eyebrow that the boy knew so well.

"You know what I mean. I'm not their real kid. Heck, I'm not even a real pug."

Bertrand slid his scaly turtle arm around the boy's neck. "Have you any idea what your name means?" He gave the boy a knowing stare. "Do you know why you're called Artemis?"

"'Cause it's my name. What are you talking about, old man?"

"Artemis was the child of Zeus, the god of all gods in Greek mythology," Bertrand said. "Artemis was the protector of wild animals and children. Your mother wanted you to have this name because she felt strongly that you protected her until she could bring you into the world."

"I protected her? Are you feeling well? Do you need to lie down?"

"Your mother left everything behind on her way here," Bertrand said. "The only thing she brought was you. She believed that if you were safe, everything was going to be right in the world."

Artemis didn't remember the short time he'd spent with his mother, but he'd heard all the stories about her. He knew she was brave and special and loving.

"When she met your folks, and me and Sarah, and all the different wonderful beings of this valley, she knew this was the right place. She didn't give you to us, son. She gave us to you. Artemis, protector of children and animals, you belong here. You are as much their kid as if you were born to Tinkerbelle this very minute." He turned the boy to face him. "Your problem is that you've got some responsibilities coming and you're scared."

Artemis bristled at being called out. "I'm not scared of nothing."

"You are accustomed to life the way you know it. There's you and your folks and me and this town, and now you're going to have a little brother or sister . . . and you're scared." Bertrand tussled Artie's mane the way it upset the boy. Being a teenager makes you self-conscious about your mane. This began a short wrestling match.

"You'd better be scared, old man," Artemis giggled as he bulled the giant cooter against the wall. "You'd better be scared of me . . ."

They both laughed and continued to horse around.

Bertrand was surprised by the boy's power. Finally, having broken Artie's mood, the elder sent him along to tend his family. "And by family, I mean your *real* family. Now get out of here."

Artemis walked the longest path home he could manage. The nearer he grew, the slower his steps. The sounds he could hear from inside his home weren't exactly screaming, but a kind of weeping that draws you closer without looking. It was Tinkerbelle for certain, although she'd never made sounds like this before. At this moment, Artie could never remember anything but love coming from his sweet mother pug.

He wasn't frightened and he wasn't saddened either, but he felt a rush of emotion. He very much wanted to gore something. His momma was crying, and he'd fight the world to protect her.

When Artemis peeked inside, his adoptive father crushed him in a teary embrace. Snuffy was simultaneously laughing and crying in a blubbering never found in nature.

He could barely speak, and yet he couldn't stop. "Oh, Artemis, my beautiful pug, Artemis . . ." Snuffy slobbered. "They're almost here . . . our new children . . . you're gonna have a brother, maybe a sister . . . maybe both." Snuffy contorted in a laughing cry on that one. "Mother," he said to Tinkerbelle, who was breathing and writhing in pain. "Do you think it could be both?" Without waiting for a response, he virtually leaped onto Artie again. "Oh wouldn't it be wonderful, boy?"

Tinkerbelle drew Artemis to her with her look and warmly embraced him. She was panting heavily, one moment smiling with great calmness, the next stressed by the enormous effort to birth her babies.

Artemis had overheard this called labor, and it seemed the perfect word.

Suddenly, Tinkerbelle grabbed the boy tightly and squelched up her face in the most abnormal way. She let go a low roar, and then, there it was. A tiny, gooey, wrinkled-up girl pug.

Snuffy pulled Artemis aside as Tink began to tend to the child. She checked and cleaned and nuzzled her pup, and finally nosed her to a feeding. Artemis didn't want to see but couldn't look away. He closed his eyes for a minute and when he opened them again, two brand-new baby pugs were furiously feeding at their momma's teats.

"You're a big brother now," Tinkerbelle said, showing Artemis how the pups had yet to even open their eyes. "From the very first, they'll be looking to you for help and love."

Artie wished there was a way to describe how simultaneously captivated and disgusted he felt. Also, overwhelmed with a sense of belonging, of kinship, of responsibility to the family that had taken him in as their own. He, too, felt an odd sense of accomplishment, although he hadn't done anything, for being more in a family now than before. And he couldn't help feeling quite superior—for the last ten minutes, he'd been a big brother twice over.

Artemis had always felt different and out of place, worried that his peers judged him for being adopted. He mostly kept to himself because he didn't make friends easily, and everyone his age intimidated him.

When he saw the mule brothers on his way home from the water project, he grew shy and self-conscious. Mules are tall to begin with, and these brothers had a sarcastic way about them that always made Artie feel like he'd missed a day of school. They were solemn and dutiful around their dad, Moe, but always goofing otherwise, which made Artemis think they were phony, and a little dangerous.

"Hey, Artemis," Matt said as he approached. "Whatcha got for snacks?"

Artie didn't have any snacks, and being asked got his guard up. "Nothing," he replied. "What kind of snacks are you looking for?"

"Oh, we got plenty for ourselves," Sam said. "Maybe too much. We were looking to trade for some of yours."

Artie softened a little. He did love a snack, and although he didn't want to know these boys, they were being friendly. Sam stepped toward Artie and slung a sack off his back. A collection of fat red berries spilled out.

"We've been eating these all day," Matt said with a satisfied grin. "Take a taste if you like."

Artie paused suspiciously.

"Go ahead," Matt cajoled. "They ain't gonna bite you back." Both mules gave toothy grins of encouragement.

As Artie leaned down and took a berry, the brothers held their breath, trying not to laugh. Artie gobbled the fruit, smacked his lips, and said thanks.

The mule brothers were stunned. "Wait a minute," Matt and Sam hollered together. "How'd ya like that berry?"

"It's good," Artie said with a straight face. "Juicy. Thanks again."

Matt took a small bite of the next berry and began to buck and spit.

Sam stifled a laugh and eyeballed Artemis like he had three heads. "You don't think these things are sour?" he demanded while his brother gagged and spat.

Artemis felt the sting of shame warm his ears again. "I don't, I mean, I can't . . ." Artie was sorry he'd ever talked to them. "I don't know what that is."

The mule boys bucked and snorted and laughed an uncomfortably long time. Artie began to size up the rude punks for a thumping, when they both knelt their heads to the ground and smiled at the steaming hog.

"That's the greatest thing I've ever seen," Matt cried.

"You're amazing," chortled Sam.

"We can't eat these things," the boys howled together, unable to catch their breath. "Nobody can."

"Nobody except you!" Matt howled. "Please, take another."

Artie munched the fruit as they tried to describe sour.

"It's like your face wants to collapse inside your mouth," Sam said through tears of laughter.

Finally, the boys disclosed their gag, telling Artie how the berries grew by the shore, and they carry them everywhere in hopes of finding a new victim. Artie gobbled a few more and laughed with his new friends, who were still rolling with glee. Artie was their hero, and an absolute necessity for their con game—he couldn't taste sourness at all.

Artie became part of the crowd. He was a big brother in a network of big brothers, dedicated to bending the will of the world to their amusement. He had his own crash test dummies at home as his pug brother Moose and sister Molly were constantly in his charge. Artie loved playing with them and teaching them new things, but he also delighted in being revered as an all-knowing elder. Old Uncle Bertrand had put him through a gag or two in his time, and Artie had gleaned a fine sense of where to place the guardrails.

Once, he secreted Moose and Molly to the sacred grounds of the Scratching Tree. "For thousands of years, humanity has tried to grasp the awesome power of this dark and gnarly haunted tree. Bird spirits have been trying to escape its evil spell for generations. Their souls are trapped and must grant the wishes of anyone who can climb her." Artie made his voice deep and spooky. "If you can conquer this tree, you will command these spirits forever."

He grew loud at the end, and the children gasped and jumped.

"But try and fail," he continued slowly and breathily, "and suffer the scratching curse."

Molly wanted no part of the game, but Moose was only too ready to win the prize. The older kids scampered along the narrow path of dead brown leaves and cajoled young Moose through the ripe patch of poison ivy. Letting perfectly good toxic shrubs go to waste made no sense at all. Artemis was an apt and able student of the art of benevolent torture for little brothers.

Moose caught a terrible itch, and Tinkerbelle had a different take on the gag. She made it clear that the boy's rear end would be like a summer breeze compared to what she'd do to Artie if he ever had another funny idea. "Just get out of my sight," she seethed, "and let me tend to your brother."

Artie felt appropriately shamed and took a slow walk to the lake. A brace of ducks were competing for the longest glide and the highest rooster across the water. Artie knew that ducks were excellent at scooting across a lake and blasting water behind them. They called it roosterbutt, and the technique was all about speed on the approach. It made for quite a show. They could also lean their butts and send the spray in different directions. Recognizing this as an opportunity to soak a little brother cheered up Artie fast. It was an excellent gag that would dry with no sign of mischief. He ran off to discuss it with the boys.

Snuffy took a stand against Pugville over Moose's rash. They really got into it. Snuffy decided it was one more reason they had to find their way home while Tinkerbelle was left to defend a hurtful prank on her own child. She was incensed. Snuffy was defensive. He had a nagging dread that he was shirking some responsibility, like he was breaking a promise to his younger self to be true to a thing he didn't completely understand. They argued for a long time.

"Do you think he's really out there?" Tinkerbelle shouted Snuffy down about finding his lousy brother.

Snuffy didn't want to admit that he was more worried about a wicked relation than his own children. "I'm sure that Tuffy is alive and has the old neighborhood to himself just like he always wanted." It was a weak argument, but the best Snuffy could manage.

"That would be nice," Tinkerbelle volleyed. "He should be well, live a long life, and die alone."

"Nice talk," Snuffy hissed, "You're a real humanitarian."

"Maybe," Tink said, lowering her voice for extra emphasis, "maybe we should live for the moment and leave the past where it is. Alive or dead, you are not your brother's keeper. You don't owe him anything."

Snuffy glared back at her in silence. He knew she was right, but he hated how he couldn't feel that way.

CHAPTER SIX

Reconnaissance

Tuffy took Crock on the long walk to the observation platform on the hill. He could see the progress of the salvage and restoration work clearly from the vantage point, and it looked like the place was turning from color to black and white. Blocks of houses policed and restored made an orderly run into the ruin and detritus of those not yet attended to.

Tuffy agonized over the fate of his little brother, Snuffy, and the girl Tinkerbelle. He felt a paternal duty to them both, confounded by feelings for the girl that he'd never quite understood. It was this anxiety that kept Tuffy focused on rebuilding the wreckage of their old home. It was his reason for keeping Anarkey and cousins working and well-fed. He hoped his family would walk back over the same hill by which they'd disappeared. And when they did, Tuffy wanted them to walk safely into the perfect community.

They climbed to the observation deck the hogs had built. It was a comfortable platform high on the clearing and secluded inside a weeping willow tree. From inside the foliage it was easy to see out, but difficult to see in from the outside and impossible from any distance. The hogs had done a fine job, and Tuffy had Roach's crew wrangle a month's worth of hay and grain as payment. While food was difficult for the hogs to find, it was a day at the beach for an insect. Tuffy continued to find jobs for the hog family as a way to keep them from stealing. He also admired anyone who bent the rules to provide for his family, and thought Anarkey a fine protégé to train as his own. Tuffy always had an angle.

Aaron and Karen were Tuffy's flying spies, grandchildren of the old duck. Aaron was a fit and muscular duck who bobbed his head while he walked, like he could hear music. He had a way of manipulating his wing feathers to look like he talked with his hands, and when he talked, he was terribly hip. Karen was a surfer chick with long black eyelashes and a bandana around her neck. She was ultra-mellow and quiet in a happy way that calmed a place when she was present. Being teenagers made them hard to understand, being hip surfers made it nearly impossible.

"Okay, dude, here's the poop," Aaron began, and already Tuffy was struggling to keep up. "The water bends back leeward. Toward the old grind after the hill."

"The . . . grind?" Tuffy felt a hundred years old.

"The old grind house, dude. By the train tracks?" Aaron played out his descriptions as if communicating in a foreign language.

"The train tracks?" Tuffy had never seen a train. "Where is that?"

"Ain't no is." He chuckled. "That train is oh-deep-thirty, brah."

Tuffy nodded slowly but did not understand.

"Real shame too," Aaron added.

Karen seemed sad too. "Right," she added sympathetically.

Tuffy tried a little pantomime in return. "So . . . the train tracks . . . are under . . . the water?" he asked as he concocted his own sign language.

"Oh, absolutely, dude," Karen piped up. "But if you bank right after the grind, go about ten clicks over the new water to the hill on the other side where the old water, you know, was, you know, before the new water, the only water . . ."

Tuffy's face contorted in pain.

Aaron listened carefully and nodded his concurrence.

"Except, of course, ya know . . . , until you get to the water . . . ," Karen finished.

"Exactamundo, dude." Aaron confirmed. "Hey, you don't want us looking around the water-water, do you?"

Tuffy stood stone-faced, barely breathing.

"You know, the ocean . . . water," Aaron looked closely at the petrified Tuffy. "Dude?"

"Don't . . . care . . . what . . . water," Tuffy answered, panting hard and also barely breathing. "Looking for pug dogs."

"Oh, right. Them. They're totally out there, dude. The pug-dog-dude and a babe-dog, dude. The ones you were looking for, Broham. And there's tonnage more, all kinds of different dudes, brah."

Tuffy celebrated the news that Snuffy and Tinkerbelle were alive. He gave himself the highest credit for being right all along. A pug has superior instincts. He was absolutely sure he wouldn't survive much more of this conversation, so he graciously made arrangements to meet again soon.

As Tuffy walked away, the ducks called after him. Tuffy hunched his shoulders as if being beaten. He slowly turned back to his confidants and managed a tortured smile. "Yes?"

"That Snuffy dude has a pair of kickers, brah."

"Kickers?" Tuffy was hoping for clarification, or maybe considering leaping to his death. He wasn't really sure. "What in the name of . . . what's a kicker?"

"Rugrats, bro, sand kickers. You know, *child-dren*." Aaron spoke as if talking to an infant. "With the pug babe Tinkerbelle."

This information landed like a ton of bricks. Tuffy sat where he'd stood. Children. Puppies. Nephews. He had to steady himself a moment, and then hastened back to the ducks. "Tell me everything," he said directly and with a laser focus. "Leave out no detail, please."

The group sat once more, and the ducks did a fine job of painting a worthy picture of Snuffy's community.

"They call it Pugville?" Tuffy was stunned.

"There's a sign and everything, brah."

CHAPTER SEVEN

Science

Snuffy was working with Bertrand on some kind of water experiment that was frankly over his head. The turtle had a remarkably long cord made from skinny leaves that he'd wound through and around the countless markers pounded into the shallow water off the beach. It was impossibly complicated, but seemed to make perfect sense to the turtle.

As they worked, Snuffy confided in Bertrand about his running argument with Tinkerbelle. "I don't want to be stuck in Pugville forever, but she wants a stable home," he said. "I want that too, but I have to know what happened back home. It's been so long, my brother could have survived the storms and still be dead already."

"I know just how you feel, my friend," Bertrand said. "My thing is to walk the earth searching for knowledge and helping others. I don't put down roots, but I always want to drift where I'm needed."

"Then help me," Snuffy pleaded. "I have to find a way home."

"Well," Bertrand pontificated, "every water that rises surely recedes, so it has to be that in time we'll see connecting land. That should reveal a path back home."

"Can we count on that?"

"No." Bertrand shot Snuffy his look of ancient wisdom. "But I'll keep working on it."

Bertrand increased his focus on mapping the island. He also was interested in discovering all things indigenous to the new place. He had a great research partner in Sarah, whom he found extraordinarily knowledgeable. He had a huge crush on her, too, even if he didn't know it.

They started their mornings before dawn to track the sun's crossing. They walked the beach at all hours, hammering posts with different coded flags on them to measure the sun and the moon and if there were any tides on the water along the beachfront. This information would provide a scientific basis for locating the island—and finding Snuffy's way home.

They spent much time foraging the woods, gathering different food and therapeutic flora. They got into a habit of enjoying afternoon picnics to pass the time before sundown, when they'd relax on a sandbar and share stories and theories about science, philosophize about learning and growing, and spin yarns about their explorations.

Bertrand had been alone so long that he had no natural ability to measure the romantic connection growing between them. He found Sarah as playful as she was serious and intelligent. It was a confounding mix that drew Bertrand close, even if he didn't really understand his own feelings. She loved to clack her claws across the turtle's hard shell in a rhythm of island music, which Bertrand found soothing and invigorating. Sometimes the sunshine and the water and the friendship made Bertrand feel giddy and bold. If only he knew what it all meant.

Her companionship was consistent and warm, which might betray an interest, but she was also a colleague, which might explain the closeness. Bertrand found her intelligence fascinating, and her femininity soothing. He was wise, but totally lost in affairs of the heart. Bertrand was also keeping a secret: he hadn't told Sarah of their biggest connection, that he was also sometimes a bear.

One afternoon as they sat and clacked, Bertrand settled back in the sand so far he was mostly on his back. The soft conversation and warm company caused a stirring inside him, a comfort and peace that was unlike anything he understood. Bertrand was falling in love.

He began to panic. It felt the same as before his transformations, which remained beyond his control.

His blood pressure was rising. His breathing was shortened, and he felt slightly fevered. He feared he was transforming into a bear, and doing it right in front of Sarah. He had to beat it out of there fast. His heart sank to think she'd feel frightened or betrayed and never speak to him again. And worst of all, he couldn't be sure that he wouldn't harm her.

He frantically tried to rise, but he couldn't move. He was inclined too far backward and settled so far into the sand that he couldn't get up. He was stuck upside-down. He knew that he needed to calm himself to escape calamity, but he couldn't do that either. The transformation was coming. He panicked further, which would only hasten the event, which panicked him all the more.

Sarah noticed his discomfort and leaned in closer to him. Bertrand squeezed shut his eyes and braced for disaster.

A very long minute passed, and nothing happened. He didn't transform. Realizing this calmed him in the way that always brought him back to his natural state. More time passed in uncomfortable silence. Bertrand finally decided it was time for full disclosure—he'd simply explain his transformations to the bear who had grown to mean everything to him.

She listened. She didn't run away or react badly. She quietly understood. She claimed knowledge of his condition, and explained her understanding that such a transition can't happen to a turtle on his back. "Almost nothing can happen when a turtle's on his back," she said cheerfully.

Bertrand was flooded with emotion. He'd never before felt so accepted and included. In that moment, he saw Sarah in a new and important way, a way he'd see her for the rest of time.

Sarah just gave the old man a soft kiss on his cheek as she helped him to his feet.

CHAPTER EIGHT

Action

Tuffy drew a rough map of Pugville Valley by translating information from surfer-duck to English. Next, he needed transportation. The neighborhood was filled with stray dogs coming home, and he commissioned a few burrowing and climbing rodents to work with them. He bound them to secrecy with some inventive blarney and challenged them to fashion any kind of boat.

After surprisingly little time, the crew had fabricated a small fleet of horrible-looking scows. The flat bottoms were countertops or bedroom doors, and broomsticks or rakes held large articles of clothing for sails. Ribbons and twine served as ropes, and ran through doorknobs and cabinet handles for hardware. Plastic of every description was stuffed everywhere possible to prevent leaking. In theory, they'd work as boats, but no one was willing to take one on the water—no one except one grizzled ferret called Bones.

Bones was lithe and strong, his fur thick and matted around his face and shoulders but soft and fluffy down his back and tail. Bones was a no-nonsense kind of polecat and wasn't one to shy away from a challenge.

The builder group slid one rickety craft to the water's edge. Bones took a running start off the beach, leaped with all his might onto the deck, and sent the thing skimming onto the water. He grabbed hold of the sail, leaned back, and swung the dress shirt into the wind. Collars and cuffs began slapping wildly, and he was underway. Then the thing picked up speed. Bones slammed all his weight to the starboard, and the boat came around. He pulled hard to port, and the boat slowed as the sail emptied. Then suddenly the shirt-sail caught the wind again and off Bones went, this time even faster.

The ferret was whooping up quite a racket, soon echoed by the group on shore. As Bones managed the rig back to land, the entire assemblage clamored for a chance at the helm. Everyone hurried to launch the other floaters and spent the rest of the day launching and sailing. Many improvements were implemented, and the rigs got much better. Tuffy suddenly had a navy.

The boats, though, had no names. This was an ongoing point of consternation among the new sailors, some of whom thought it necessary even though they had no idea why. Finally, Bones named his vessel *The Swift*. It wasn't christened or painted on the float, but it became her name.

Bones knew that swift meant fast, and he liked the idea that his floater was fast.

Bones had fallen into a partnership of sorts with a particular chipmunk. They were sailing and making improvements together, and they worked well as a team. The chipmunk was called Earl, which made you ask if he was a squirrel, a topic that can make a chipmunk sensitive. Bones couldn't care less about it, and frankly wouldn't know one from the other anyway. They were both sure that their float was swift, and that was good enough basis for friendship.

Tuffy recruited several Labradors for his new venture, Labradors being helpful and loyal, and great swimmers. One large golden Lab was called Otter, and he loved to be asked why. "Because I'm *Otter* than you are," he'd say, laughing every time.

The crews practiced sailing for a few days, then decided it was time to find the other side of the water. After every boat was loaded, Otter jumped in the water to guide the launch. When the last was off, he jumped in with Bones and Earl. Bones caught a breeze in the big dress shirt, and off they sailed.

The crews had vowed to stay close together, to look after one another. They vowed to help any one of them who was in distress. It was a code of honor among sailors. This was their solemn promise.

So as soon as Bones found the wind, *The Swift* was off like a bolt of lightning, leaving the others hollering in its wake.

Earl had memorized Tuffy's map. He insisted chipmunks were known for their flawless memories, a claim no one could dispute. He knew which landmarks to anticipate, but surrounded by water, he'd resorted to guessing and trying to read directions by the sun.

Hours passed. Bones was placated by a fine wind that he kept well in his sail. Otter was just happy to be out for a ride.

But they were all growing concerned they were hopelessly lost. Otter began eyeing the provisions, building a case in his head for more food because he was the largest animal. Earl started making up stuff to cover for being lost, which prompted loud arguments from Bones.

"I can't see anything you're talking about . . . and neither can you."

"When I'm navigating, pay attention or we're lost out here for sure!" Earl shouted back.

"I'm paying attention to being lost at sea, ya moron."

If nothing else, the bickering killed a lot of time.

The two were in the middle of another argument about a landmark tree that nobody could possibly see, when Otter began slowly and quietly interrupting.

"Whoa . . . ," he intoned. "Hey, hey, fellas . . ."

"Don't tell me you can see a giant oak," Bones said, in full-throated disagreement. "You wouldn't know a giant oak if it was dating your mom."

"My *mom*!" A vein was nearly bursting out of the chipmunk's head. "Lissen, ya freak of a tall *rat*, don't *ever* tell a chipmunk about an oak tree, and my mom was the dearest, sweetest . . ."

"*Fellas!*" Otter wished to be heard. "It's there. I see land over there."

They all stopped yelling long enough to look, and there it was indeed. *The Swift* had navigated the waters beyond the old neighborhood.

The crew made land. Bones and Otter stretched out on a soft patch of moss and shade while the chipmunk, honoring a true act of karma, was collecting acorns from the giant oak right above them. He couldn't wait to share them with the boys. He couldn't wait to remind Bones of this oak tree every day for the rest of his life.

The next order of business was to find the valley. There was a long stretch of shoreline that bent out of sight, and there was the hill that climbed into the woods. They agreed to walk along the shore looking for an easier climb. Earl remembered the map had a lake at the end of a mountain stream, so they'd be climbing eventually. Still, the boys wanted to see the shoreline.

Bones spotted another makeshift boat along the shore to the west. Otter recognized Cubbie, a squirrel who'd helped him tie lines during the building party. He'd sailed with Luke, another Labrador the boys remembered from the building gang. As they caught up to the new crew, the sun was sinking low in the sky.

They set up for the night. They built a big fire, and Earl discussed at length the virtue of roasting or not roasting acorns. He made a point of standing near Cubbie the squirrel to consider these questions, if only to prove how different and unique were chipmunks.

Bones scavenged a variety of food from the nearby vegetation, and the group spent a fine night bonding over stories and laughter.

Morning came early, and the intrepid sailors rose to begin the day. The fire was tended, breakfast was scavenged, and the dogs took a dip in the water. Otter spotted a formation of ducks loudly quacking their way toward the island. They all watched as the formation moved toward them, then circled back and flew toward them again.

"Their leader is flying on one wing," Bones declared. "See how they always circle to the right?"

"Why in the world would they have the broken bird fly out front?" Earl asked.

"Maybe cuz he memorized the map . . . so they're lost for sure . . ."

"*Hey*, I got us here. Where are we now, smart guy? Huh? You still lost, you little . . . ?"

"*Fellas!*" Once again Otter poked his nose into the argument as the voice of reason. "Look, on the water. Below the birds."

Everyone looked to see what Otter had seen. And there on the water was a giant pajama shirt, filled with wind and blowing toward them. It was the other crew, led by a formation of ducks.

Bones slapped his forehead.

"That is the most sensible thing I've seen in weeks," he said, mainly to insult Earl, who blew him a raspberry behind his back.

Cubbie scurried up a tree to signal their location, while Luke and Otter killed time playing in the water. Bones and Earl sat squabbling on the beach.

Jack and Cookie sailed straight to the beach. Jack was a Jack Russell terrier and Cookie a springer spaniel, medium-sized dogs with pronounced snouts and waggly tails. They had similar dark and rusty brown patches on their backs and legs and might have been mistaken for brothers except a terrier's fur is short and wiry while a spaniel's is longer and silkier.

Both Jack and Cookie were smart and capable dogs. They landed their rig at the campsite, and all pitched in to hide the boats, put out the fire, and police the grounds.

"Before we shoved off from the other side of this water," Jack said, "I had a nice long talk with Tuffy and the ducks. The valley we're looking for is just behind this next stretch of coastline." Jack had been a movie dog in his life with people, and his résumé boasted seventy-five different tricks he could do on demand and for the camera. Jack felt this experience would make him a good team leader, and he said so. "We should probably climb this hill to the stream above the lake. That way, we'll look like we've arrived through the woods and not the water."

It was the kind of complex reasoning one could expect from a movie dog, and most of the crew was glad to have Jack there to help. Bones thought it sounded like a lot of extra work, and Earl immediately began saying nasty things about Bones. An unsurprising argument ensued, and once again Otter stepped between them. The crew of *The Swift* was bonding nicely.

They climbed the hill and found the stream. Then they split up so they would look less suspicious when they arrived in town.

Songbirds began singing their arrival, welcoming strangers across the valley. Bones and Earl went into the woods to meet the squirrels and chipmunks. They were greeted as family and given a tour. They surreptitiously collected names and locations of everyone in Pugville.

Jack and Cookie kept to the perimeter and took notes on the geography of the valley. They'd agreed to take care not to bump into Snuffy or Tinkerbelle and spoil Tuffy's surprise of a practical joke and family reunion. They actually thought it such a great idea that they pitched in and helped form the plan.

The Labradors, Luke and Otter, went straight to the lake and played with the ducks and the children. Labradors are well-known water dogs, and they enjoyed watching the rooster-butting ducks. They even helped soak a kid or two. Sheriff Buck stopped them for a few questions, but gave more information than he received. Pugville always had new friends finding their way to the valley, so the spies didn't raise any alarm.

They all left in different directions while the sun was still high, and had a short and direct sail back across the water. They even spotted the Pugville sign at the edge of town.

Tuffy paced furiously and listened attentively to every detail of every report. He took careful notes and cross-examined each sailor for precise descriptions of everything.

These details confirmed that his goofy little brother hadn't the good sense to be in charge of anything. He didn't know the first thing about responsible leadership. In Tuffy's estimation, the little pug had learned nothing from growing up with people and was a danger to himself and to others.

The sailing crews made many more trips and always reported back to a stern and sullen Tuffy. Word began to leak throughout the neighborhood about the place across the water. Stories circulated that there was a place for all pugs to do as they wished, and where everyone was a pug. Tuffy, Snake, and the boys pooh-poohed the idea, but Pugville was becoming a real thing in the imagination of all those working the neighborhood.

Then Bones and the crew posted a sarcastic sign by the shore that made Pugville more real than ever. The sailors wouldn't admit to the joke, but everyone was proud of it. The sign read as follows:

THUGVILLE

Population: unknown

Tuffy did not order the sign removed. He had a better idea to assure his place of respect and authority in the neighborhood. He calmly gathered Crock, Snake, and Mole, and took a friendly walk across the neighborhood. When they arrived at the correct house, Tuffy knocked at the same time he opened the door. A startled opossum tending her kids jumped at the intrusion.

"Calm down," Tuffy said in a terrifyingly measured voice, "where's your husband?"

The opossum couldn't speak for fear but managed to nod inside. Mole and Snake searched the place. Moments later they returned with the husband and a small box of insignificant jewelry.

"Out. Get out!" Tuffy shouted at the woman, who sobbed knowing what kind of trouble this was. "Take your children and get out." The mother and her children scrambled for the door. She paused to look back at her husband, and saw him mouth the words, 'I'm sorry' through his own tears.

A few moments later, Tuffy exited the house carrying the box of jewels. Tuffy had made Mole give the possum a beating because it was Mole's guy who stole from him. Tuffy found the wife and kids cowering near the house.

"If this was a misunderstanding, like your man says it was…" Tuffy said.

"It was!!" she interrupted, crying, "it was…"

"If it was," Tuffy continued, "if it was then it's all over now and we can go back to being friends." The wife began to bawl out loud and Tuffy comforted her. "It's all right," he soothed, "it's okay. Now you know not to do this again. Now go inside, everybody's all right."

The woman shooed her kids inside, more frightened than ever.

Word spread quickly that Thugville was more than just a joke painted on a shabby sign.

CHAPTER NINE

Founders' Day

Pandora Peahen was busy preparing the monthly report in her delightful little space near the town square. She had a long, hollow trough for filing, with flat dried leaves for paper. She had a heavily barked tree in her office where she posted important reminders with thorns, next to a perfectly round trunk she used as a desk. Her routine included regular indexing of Pugville homes and businesses, and she chaired a monthly meeting to report city business and hear from citizens.

As she reviewed her research, Pandora stopped dead in her tracks. She checked her math twice, set down her paper, and ran to find Snuffy.

"Oh, Mr. Mayor!" Pandora was out of breath when she caught up to Snuffy at the mules' place. "Mr. Mayor, great news."

Snuffy and Moe were checking out a newly engineered mule harness.

"What is it?" Snuffy asked.

"One thousand!" Pandora said excitedly. "The town has just reached one thousand."

"Welp," Moe said, sporting the biggest grin imaginable. "That's quite a number."

The three jumped and danced in celebration.

"A party." Moe sat down on his haunches at the great idea. "We must have a party."

"Well, sure," Snuffy said, although he wasn't sure at all. "A party's a good idea."

"In the town square," Moe said.

"The town square is so big for a party," Snuffy said.

"Doggone it," Moe said effusively. "The darn town's a thousand 'n we're gonna have us a party."

Moe kicked his front legs this way and that, and Pandora danced with him.

Snuffy wasn't sure if he was up to the task of organizing a party. He didn't like the idea of choosing for others, and a party had food and a time and place, and a lot of stuff people should decide for themselves. Snuffy thought the mayor asking you to a party meant you couldn't say no. Snuffy wasn't going to be comfortable with that. He thanked Pandora for the news, gave Moe a slap on the rear, and set off to confer with Tinkerbelle.

The news traveled faster than he did, and soon everybody was congratulating him and volunteering ideas for the party. They stopped him in the street to describe how they had the perfect decorations. The squirrels found him at home to say they could build and set a great table. The songbirds gathered to report how they'd be thrilled to sing if Snuffy could organize a stage.

And then Bertrand showed up with the most harrowing idea of all. "It should be a Founders' Day—the town should honor you and Tinkerbelle, and it should happen once a year," Bertrand opined in a learned and superior way. "This is a thing we should absolutely do."

"That's it," Snuffy declared emphatically. "There will be no party. Not now, not ever."

Three weeks later on a beautiful spring morning, the town buzzed in anticipation of its first Founders' Day.

"To pay tribute to good people working together and celebrate the milestone of reaching population one thousand," Mayor Snuffy proclaimed authoritatively. "And that's all."

The mayor had spoken.

Early on the morning of the party, Snuffy called Artemis to his side. "You're nearly a full-grown hog, my pug. I want to ask you to do something very important, something I wouldn't trust to just anybody. Go to the edge of town this morning and be back in time for the party. Can you do it?"

Artemis nodded, and Snuffy handed him his ceremonial paint kit.

"Please update our sign to reflect our new population. It's a great honor I'm asking you."

"I understand, Dad. Thank you."

Artemis knew the significance of the gesture. To update his father's landmark was a sober undertaking. He also knew that everywhere he went, his little brother went too. Artemis and Moose were no different from most siblings in that the big brother was ever courting trouble and the younger always foreboding consequences. Today would be no different. Artemis took the materials and started off, Moose quickly by his side.

"Can I hold the paints?" Moose asked immediately.

This was going to be a long walk if the kid had an endless supply of stupid questions, Artemis thought, and the kid always had an endless supply of stupid questions. "When we get there," was his rote response. "We can't risk spilling Dad's stuff on the way."

Moose continued to barrage his big brother with simplistic inquiries that made Artemis's head feel like it might explode.

"How far is it? How do different paints get to be different colors? How long does it take to dry?"

Artemis always delved into a kind of fugue state whenever he was alone with his brother, from which he could answer and not really consider the torrent of questions at the same time. It was during one of these trances that Artemis failed to immediately notice the two strangers who were suddenly walking beside them. It was Luke and Otter, the two big Labradors.

"Hey," Artemis said after a minute. "I recognize you guys from the lake, don't I?"

"Of course you do," Luke said. "Whatchoo guys up to?"

"Aww, my goofy little brother and I have to paint the sign at the edge of town."

"Don't know much about painting," Otter volunteered. "But maybe we can help carry something."

Artemis wasn't sure why he knew that Labradors loved to carry things, but he did, and so the offer sounded quite normal.

"Town's a thousand," Moose declared. "We get to change the number."

"Thousand's a big number," Luke said, and off they went.

They carried on together, stopping along the way to trick Moose into sniffing an old skunk hole and stepping into soft dung. Artemis was truly happy for the company and for the mischief he could deny having conjured. Artemis was also protective of his little bro, sometimes voting down a prank as too dangerous. This helped Moose feel protected. Everyone was having a great time.

Snuffy was especially nervous as he prepared for the festival. He was most comfortable when he could just agree with people and not make choices for them. He had Moe and the boys come early to pull the giant feast to the town square. He checked and rechecked every detail and was as ready as he'd ever be. He kissed Molly and Tinkerbelle goodbye and walked with the mule boys to finish the preparations.

Just before they rounded the bend, Snuffy nudged Bertrand to point out the black smoke rising above the thick canopy by the water. As they stared in confusion, a hellish commotion erupted by the lake, with splashing, barking, growling, and howling.

As if they could read one another's mind, Bertrand and Snuffy said simultaneously, "I'll go this way, you go there." Snuffy bolted toward the shore, and Bertrand hustled toward the lake.

The wind was blowing rancid plumes of black smoke straight into Snuffy's face. It smelled of rubber and plastic, like the stench of dead people's feet. The celebrants of Founders' Day were being blinded and suffocated, coughing, gagging, and choking. Everyone was running away and taking cover. Children were getting lost and trampled and screaming for their parents. Wails of panic and fear came from every direction.

Bertrand hit the lake surrounded by big, happy dogs. They jumped and splashed in celebration and knocked the old man around. He was dunked and lapped, wrestled and chased, and couldn't find his way out of the middle.

Meanwhile, Bones and Earl strolled calmly through the mayhem. They had a detailed description of a girl pug to grab and take back home. They were to look for her at the town square and follow the path to her house until they found her. The instructions were foolproof. Cubbie joined them, also according to plan. Three innocent rodents out for an afternoon stroll.

Tuffy had made it abundantly clear that under no circumstances were they to hurt the girl, and because they were returning her to her original home, they'd be heroes. It wasn't a crime, and it wasn't mean. It was just a harmless prank on a relative. The other goofy pug they could leave behind to be retrieved at another time, Tuffy had said. He'd coordinated every phase of the operation to the last detail. If everybody did their job, the game was won. These were Tuffy's instructions. These were Tuffy's own words.

The three skeevy conspirators searched all the way to Snuffy's house, then split up to find the girl. It didn't take much to bring Tink out with a frying pan, ready to wallop anybody who got within arm's reach. She met Bones at the front porch.

"Whoa, girl, nobody's going to hurt you . . ." Bones approached slowly with his ferret claws low. "That's right. Just give old Bones the pan, and everything'll . . ."

Bones didn't have time to finish his thought before Tinkerbelle brained him. The blow shot him clean off the porch.

Earl and Cubbie jumped in to drag Bones away by his hair, offering words of surrender to Tinkerbelle. "Okay, lady. We get the message. We don't want no trouble here."

The loud clang of cookware on skull had brought Molly out of the home as well. Bones slowly regained his senses, but when he saw Molly and Tinkerbelle together, he was sure he was still dreaming.

"Hey, buddy?" he whispered to Earl. "Do you see two of the same dog?"

"I think so," was the best Earl could muster.

The three intruders retreated to safer positions.

"I got orders," Bones said, "for one girl pug of a specific description."

"Same here," Earl concurred.

Cubbie nodded his head slowly, not taking his eyes off the frying pan. "I'm seeing two girl pugs that fit that description."

"Same here," Earl quickly agreed again.

"So the way I figure it," Bones continued, "we can take the littler one or the one who cracks your head with a skillet."

"Right," Earl happily agreed again. "Then let's do this and get out of here."

Bones broke the huddle, picking up a long and narrow twig. He advanced on Tinkerbelle with a fencing lunge and parry, which was just enough to back her up while the others grabbed Molly. Both pugs howled loud enough to pierce any nearby eardrums, and Bones lunged once more, collapsing a wailing Tinkerbelle against the stoop.

As Bones turned and ran, he laughed aloud. "Girls," he said dismissively just before the frying pan hit the back of his head again. Bones tumbled forward, and in his last moments of consciousness and with all of his strength, he stumbled toward the water.

Snuffy ran past the smoky square to the fire, hightailing it through the overgrown path toward the beach. As he stormed through the thick foliage, he stepped right into a spring trap and was flung into the air, swinging upside down from his back foot. The pain was intense, but being shanghaied in a crisis hurt even worse. He was powerless while his town was under attack. Snuffy cried for help.

Cookie and Jack sniffed the path and wagged their tails innocently until they found Snuffy hanging from the trap they'd set earlier that morning. It made for an awkward reunion at best. They remembered one another from the old neighborhood, and Cookie and Jack were truly happy to see their old friend. They also realized Tuffy's orders hadn't been a harmless prank. They'd been duped. The scope of the deceit and the terror of the attack disgusted them. "How can we help?" they asked as they cut Snuffy down from the tree.

The dogs on the lake suddenly stopped playing and left as a group. Bertrand was battered and slobbered, though a happy mess. It was an assault any way you looked at it, but an assault by playful dogs still leaves you giggling. Bertrand was a little sore, and racked with fear about the smoke and fire. He hustled back to town square.

The scene there was catastrophic. Neighbors and friends stumbled over one another, frightened and suffocating. Bertrand began guiding friends to clear air while searching through the muck for any sign of Snuffy. Surrounded by misery, Bertrand's protection response was rising to transformation, but he was trying to remain calm.

On the other side of the square, Jack, Cookie, and Snuffy were helping others crawl below the smoke to fresh air. They were herding everyone they could to the outskirts of the square, handing off the lost and infirm to townsfolk who'd begun a medical triage in the grass along the hillside. Snuffy was limping heavily on his sore leg, and as he moved in the crowd, he constantly fell.

Bertrand finally spotted Snuffy and started toward him. Just then, Jack stumbled into the limping Snuffy, and Cookie reached out for both of them. What Bertrand saw was a strange dog make a tackling move toward Snuffy's legs, and as he yelped in pain, another strange dog went straight for his throat.

Bertrand transformed instantly into a ferocious bear and reached the three dogs in a few strides. He pummeled the two strangers with thunderous blows from the left and then the right. He scooped up Snuffy and leaped to a patch of clear air.

In an act of providence, a gentle rain began to fall over the valley, and a bright bolt of lightning split the sky. Within moments, a light rain was blowing across the valley, clearing the smoke from the stinky fire. The increasing drops extinguished the fire by the shore. Everybody took their first clean breaths as they pitched in to help one another. Jack and Cookie remained passed out where Bertrand had dropped them.

GENERAL STORE
OFFICE
FOU
ERS DAY

CHAPTER TEN

Panic

Moose and Artemis arrived in a fever. They knew they were coming back late for the party, but when they reached the town square and saw the smoke and confusion, they bolted for home. Hearing their mother's cries tore them apart, and Artemis was choking back his anger. He wanted to gore something, but he couldn't decide what.

Moose curled into a ball at his mother's feet, and she held him close for comfort. She didn't respond when they asked what happened. Tinkerbelle was slowly composing herself, holding her boys tightly. Artemis had a million questions, but instinctively knew just being there was the best help he could give. It felt like an eternity before Snuffy and Bertrand arrived.

Tinkerbelle leapt onto Snuffy, crying, "Molly! They took Molly! She's gone."

She collapsed again to the ground. Snuffy grabbed her tight, and in a controlled panic, Tinkerbelle shared what had happened.

"Stay here and take care of your mother," Snuffy instructed Moose.

Then the three boys bolted back to town.

Bertrand and Artemis split up to search. Bertrand found Sarah in the makeshift medical ward on the hillside and quickly apprised her of what happened. Then he took her aside and confided that the secret he'd shared with her was about to happen. For the first time in his life, he was going to transform into a bear under his own control.

Sarah hugged Bertrand and told him it made her proud and she wasn't afraid.

As he turned to go, she held him back and said, "Do it here. I want to see."

Bertrand smiled that wry and knowing smile and shut his eyes tightly. A kind of a popping sound rang out, and there he was, a big brown bear.

Sarah stood in amazement and looked deeply into his eyes. "I can see you in there, Bertrand. I can see it's you."

The words warmed his heart and distracted Bertrand so much that he felt himself beginning to transform back. A panicked recollection of why he'd transformed in the first place sent him loping into the woods.

The sailing men of Thugville returned to the sea victorious, then proudly rode their beloved vessels gloriously home. The trip was smooth for everyone except the again-conscious Bones, and Earl and Cubbie, who had a snarling, vicious pug as their special guest. They also had dire warnings of unspeakable repercussions if any harm came to her. Bones was doing his best to sail the boat with a swollen head and a blistering ache, and Molly was doing all she could to add to his misery.

"You have no idea who you've messed with now," she said, threatening him. "My big brother will have you and your little friend here for lunch . . . *and then go find your daddy*!"

She punctuated her threats with jabs and kicks, always finding the spot on Bones's skull that Tinkerbelle had tenderized.

The boys were afraid to handle her too roughly. They had her strapped to the floater, but it was more like a seat belt than a restraint. She had a lot of room for movement, particularly toward Bones's head.

"You're gonna wish you were never born," Molly continued unabated. "My brother'll beat you so bad your *momma* won't recognize you." Her raised voice alone was enough to torture the ferret, so the pokes on his noggin were just cruel.

"Hey," Bones protested through clenched teeth, "why don'tcha bang on the chipmunk for a while?"

"I'll *bang,*" (strike for emphasis), "*whomever,*" (another strike), "I *please!*" she shouted shrilly, adding another strike at the end for good measure.

"Owwww," Bones moaned, steering his sail the other direction so he could spend a minute on the opposite side of the boat from Molly. He whispered to Earl, "You think it's too late to go get the other dog?"

Tinkerbelle was breathing normally again. She gently asked Moose to tell all that he knew, all that he and Artemis had seen earlier. "Nobody is in trouble, sweetheart," she said softly, "but everything is important to share."

He relayed how he'd gone to the sign and met the friendly dogs. He shared all the new pranks they'd played on him, and how he didn't cry or run away. He said he knew they were tricks and he wasn't scared, but most of the time he was tricked anyway. "And just like you said, Momma, the other kids were just having fun with me. I was included." Moose was most proud of that.

It made his mother cry all over again.

Then Moose said they parted company with the two dogs halfway back to the square, and described the chaos they found when they returned.

"We didn't even look for Dad," Moose said. "We just started running for home. Artemis said, 'C'mon, pal, run,' and we both started running."

Bertrand and Artemis had been combing the woods in circular patterns, and finally found one another in the middle. There was no sign of Molly. They asked the songbirds, who hadn't seen her and were pretty sure she hadn't left town that way.

"So either she's still here, or she left by the east road or the water," Artie surmised.

"It couldn't be the water," Bertrand reasoned. "But it would make sense to hide up the coast. You shoot straight over the hill and search the beach back to town, and I'll come up the coast the other way until we meet." Bertrand whistled up to the trees. "Send word around to look for Molly. And would some of you please follow Artemis and call out if there's trouble?"

The birds understood and began to spread out.

Meanwhile, Snuffy and the sheriff were trying to question Cookie and Jack. They were awake but groggy, and not making much sense. Sheriff Buck raised them up in each arm and delivered them to Sarah in the medical tent.

Sarah felt around their haunches and jawbones.

"I'm not sure if anything's broken," she said. "We should let them sleep. I'll keep an eye on them."

Sheriff Buck quietly asked her to ensure they didn't disappear. Then he caught up to Pandora, and she agreed it would be helpful to start taking notes on everything anyone could remember seeing the entire day. Any information might prove useful.

Bertrand stopped running long enough to collect Snuffy. Halfway around the shore, they reached Artemis, who was nosing through the brush near a great many drag marks. Bertrand spotted remnants of a meal in the sand, and Snuffy sniffed out an old campfire. They'd found someone's campsite.

Artie cried out in foul language suddenly. He'd found a primitive boat hidden in the shrubbery. The trio dragged it out. Close examination proved the invention quite impressive for building something out of garbage. Artemis wanted to put the thing in the water despite the grown-ups' strong objections, so he climbed aboard and dry-ran the boat until he'd learned how to work the rudimentary controls. He was sure he could make it sail.

The birds that accompanied Artemis were milling about, pecking at the sand. They said they had to agree with Artie. "That boat has come across this water many times. I'm sure the boy could do it."

The friends were shocked to their cores. They quizzed the birds to confirm the unbelievable news.

"What you say, it's not a figure of speech or something you heard?" Bertrand insisted. "You've seen this thing sail across the water?"

"Many times," the birds replied.

Shocked and confused, the three stashed the floater and asked the shorebirds to look around the valley for more boats. Word spread quickly. Some encouraging leads were found, pieces that might have been a boat washed up in the shrubbery close to shore, but they all turned out to be dead ends, just junk carried into the brush back when the floods raged.

CHAPTER ELEVEN

Delivery

The second of the returning boats, the one without Molly, was overloaded, standing room only, and a giant party. Everyone laughed and swore and tussled as victors do in the service of a greater good. There was much to celebrate. They'd engineered a flotilla of sailing ships, made it to their destination, learned the terrain, and captured the prize. Surely they'd now be richly rewarded. The crew garbled out songs of seafaring men to the best of their recollection. Full-throated and horrible singing echoed off the water.

When they came within view of the shore, shouts of "Thugville, ho!" bellowed across the gulf. Rat, who had been standing guard since the boats were launched, leapt from his post and raced to tell Tuffy the news.

The craft made a reckless approach and hit the beach too quickly. Half of the riders were catapulted head over haunches onto the land. This spurred the loudest roar of laughter yet.

Tuffy arrived at the shoreline as nervous as a new dad. He wore his finest haberdashery to the rendezvous—formal vest, bowler hat, gold pocket watch, and a walking stick fit for a king. His sailors, goofy with success, embraced him and regaled him with songs and celebration. Tuffy fought through the drunken louts, looking for his prize. He searched the entire beachhead and couldn't find the girl.

Slowly, while drawing in a long breath, he returned to Rat's side. "Rat," Tuffy said, trying his best to use an inside voice. "Where's the girl?"

"The girl?" Rat scrambled as he always did when he sensed trouble. "Oh, the *girl* . . . Of course, the girl . . ." Rat was pointing around like a moron, trying to buy time. He finally just braced himself. "I dunno. What girl?"

Tuffy exploded in a rage Rat saw every day. "The girl! The *girl*! The whole reason for this entire undertaking, you little rat turd . . . *Where's the girl?*"

"Uh, not to interrupt, sir," Luke interjected, not sure if he really wanted to help. "The girl is coming with the other guys."

Tuffy looked up to see *The Swift* a hundred yards out. It was traveling at a good clip under a full sail, and just then the high-pitched squawking of the young pug reached their ears. Bones was still at the helm, and his faithful crewmates,

Cubbie and Earl, were carefully hunkered out of Molly's reach.

The floater was approaching way too quickly, until at the last moment, Bones slammed the vessel hard to one side and drifted slowly to shore. The skier's stop threw a spray of foam high in the air, and then down on top of everyone nearby. Tuffy was drenched. His smart plaid vest was soaked through to his fur, and his favorite hat was drifting away in a surge of froth. He poked his regal scepter into the beach to catch it. He was dripping into his own puddle when Earl and Cubbie stood tall and presented the girl. Bones and his aching head came up slowly and apologized for the mess.

Tuffy and Molly both spoke at once. "Who is this?" they each asked.

"The girl you asked for," Bones said, running his paw over the lumps on his head.

"This is not the girl," Tuffy said. "You got the wrong girl."

Molly was taking a very close look at Tuffy. "I guess you run things around here?" she asked in the snarkiest tone she could manage.

Tuffy's anger subsided as he finally recognized the pup as a fantastically young version of Tinkerbelle. "I do," he said. "Do you know who I am?"

"Well, you look like my dad," Molly replied. "But you're so much older. Are you my grandpa?"

Tuffy was embarrassed, but disarmed at the same time. This child was 100 percent Tinkerbelle's, no denying it. Had anyone else in the world embarrassed him in front of subordinates, they'd be licking teeth marks for a week. But here was this young girl talking smack and still standing.

"I am your uncle, and if you don't mind, I'd like for you to be my guest."

"I guess I don't mind," she said, throwing a dirty look at Bones and Earl. "Whatcha got to eat?"

Tuffy and his goons walked Molly to the compound. He was making a big show of greeting everyone by their names, asking about wives and husbands and children, acting like the biggest man in town. Showing off for a child made Molly roll her eyes. She felt embarrassed for the old man.

Tuffy's big show ended just inside the door of the main house. He dispatched Rat to secure the girl in an upstairs bedroom. The door was locked from the outside and the windows nailed shut, but otherwise the room was clean and comfortable.

CHAPTER TWELVE

Artie's Mission

Moose wasn't happy. He was cold and damp, hunkered down on the shoreline well before dawn. He'd sworn to be brave and heroic for his family, so he was trying with all his might to keep his yap shut. Otherwise he'd be whining like a baby about a list of things—a list he'd try to save for a better time.

"Wait here for two minutes," Artemis whispered seriously. "And stay out of sight." He slipped into the brush.

Moose obscured himself inside some shrubbery that turned out to be wet and creepy. *This is definitely going on the list,* he thought.

Seconds later, Artemis returned and threw aside branches and leaves to reveal the floater he'd found a day earlier.

"Wow!" Moose exclaimed. "What is it?"

"It's a little boat, little brother," Artemis proudly responded. "And we're going to sail it."

Moose immediately felt heroic as he helped dig out the sailing machine. Pawing sand through his little haunches made him feel as though he was making a difference, like he was part of the team.

They wrestled it to the water and boarded the rescue ship.

"This is so cool!" Moose sang out. "Can I try it?"

"You hang on to the steering stick off the back. Try and keep it straight as you can until I say to steer, okay?"

"You bet." Moose was a new man, all grown, with the hopes and dreams of his generation in his little pug paws.

Artemis got a good launch off the beach, and quickly they were floating. The sails were moving okay and the thing felt stable, but they weren't moving much. They both paddled and pushed with sticks they'd found on the beach. Moose tired quickly and began to whine. Artie began to wonder if his plans were hopeless.

The dawn broke, and a chill wind hit their faces. Artemis worked the sails around until he could feel the wind entering and leaving the old clothes, and just that quickly, they were sailing. Moose immediately reanimated with the momentum.

"I talked to the shorebirds," Artie told his little mate. "They're pretty sure we should go this way."

He showed Moose how to keep the boat going straight with the piece of wood hanging off the back. Then Moose was a sailor too.

Tinkerbelle hadn't slept a wink. She was on the warpath. Her daughter had been kidnapped in a horrible assault, and now her sons had disappeared. She was a broken, angry, assertive mother who was going to get some answers.

She made a beeline to Sarah's cave. Bertrand and Sarah had long ago retired pretense and began spending nights together inside.

Tinkerbelle busted in and kicked the old man hard on his shell, startling him out of a deep sleep. "Where are my kids?" she demanded.

Bertrand was taken completely off guard. He sheepishly balked and stalled. He knew the answer but wasn't prepared for the question. It showed all over his face.

"I don't give a single hoot what kind of deal you made," Tink said in a low voice, almost a growl, "or what kind of trust you are betraying. Where are my boys?" Tinkerbelle was doing her best not to rupture a vein.

"The boys took the boat we found," Bertrand said, deciding it was best after all to get it out quickly. "They have an idea where to find Molly, and they're going after her."

Tinkerbelle exploded. "How could you let them go? They're children! When were you going to tell us about this?"

Bertrand let her vent. She had every right to her anger and frustration. After the room had cooled slightly, he finally answered. "He spoke to me as an adult. He stated his case and outlined his plan. He did not ask for permission. He asked for help."

Tinkerbelle remained unmoved.

"I was terrified, Tink, but you didn't look into the boy's eyes like I did. He wasn't staying here. He was doing this whether I agreed with him or not, which I most certainly did not."

"Where?" Tinkerbelle forced out, still trying to believe what she was hearing. "Where did he say they were going?"

Bertrand described how Artemis had deciphered the workings of the boat, how the songbirds had helped him sketch a map, how he believed his little brother was ready for the mission. "This was not a spoiled kid throwing a tantrum. He is strong, smart, and determined."

"He's a child," was all Tinkerbelle could manage before she broke down again.

"Hey, Moose, did you just turn a little and get the wind back?" Artemis asked, wrestling with the sail.

"Yup," Moose said. "I could see it move off the big jacket, so I steered to where it went."

"Because you could see the wind move?"

"Yup," said the boy, beaming with pride. "You can see which way the wind goes when you're watching."

"Way to go, little brother," Artie said, perhaps the first sincere compliment he'd ever paid the boy. "Really, that's a big help."

Moose felt ten feet tall as they began to communicate the direction of the wind, which way to trim the sail, and when to till the rudder. For the first time, they were working as a team. Moose was becoming a sailing expert, and a huge help. Artie was impressed. They had the sun in their faces and the wind at their backs on a craft that couldn't possibly be more fun to ride. For a moment, Artie almost forgot why they were out there in the first place.

Sailing the tub was a slalom, which made it fun but time-consuming. Artemis was watching the sun as much as he was watching the sail, which was slowing them down all the more. The water carried on forever in all directions, and Artie was mentally preparing himself for the possibility they'd be floating all night. Then he began thinking of all the reasons not to bring a whiny little brother on a massively uncomfortable trip. Worry was eating at Artie's concentration, and Moose began to berate him for not keeping up.

"Artie!" Moose exclaimed as he cranked the tiller hard toward the wind. "Pay attention. What are you thinking, ya big dreaming pug?"

Artemis had to chuckle at the boy taking control. *You're right,* he thought. *I missed a turn because I was worrying about keeping you alive.* He turned a wry smile toward the little captain and whipped the sail into place. The tub bolted ahead in the new breeze, and right away, Artemis felt better. Still, he had no idea where they were, and even less where they were going.

Jack and Cookie were awake and feeling better, despite their serious injuries. Bertrand apologized again, and once again, the dogs demurred. They were quite sure they deserved a good beating. They were both ashamed they'd participated in the attack.

"Also," Jack said, "you need to know how strongly I believe Molly is absolutely safe."

The words raised a few eyebrows and restarted Tinkerbelle's tears.

"Every single animal in that neighborhood knows what your brother and his friends are capable of," Jack continued. "And he made it clear . . . he made it very clear that no harm will come to the girl."

"And those rodent thugs—they understood that?" Tinkerbelle asked, turning from sadness to anger.

"They understand being eaten by Tuffy's alligator buddy, and how that would be the most pleasant part of their day. They understand."

The conversation stopped as everyone imagined Tuffy with an alligator.

"So what do they want?" Snuffy asked. "Why did this happen?"

"That might be the worst part of the whole story," Jack said, hanging his head. "There's no way we came here to get your daughter . . ." He couldn't continue.

An intense silence gripped the group, and slowly they all understood the words Jack couldn't bring himself to say. It was supposed to be Tinkerbelle.

Snuffy's face turned to stone as he squeezed Tinkerbelle from behind. "It's my fault," he whispered. "This is my fault. I did this."

Tinkerbelle wasn't sure she'd heard correctly.

"Tuffy was right. We never should have climbed over that hill. What was I thinking?"

Tink turned around to face Snuffy.

He began to cry. "I can't do this, choose for others, be a mayor, I wasn't made for this . . ."

"Don't be silly," Tinkerbelle said softly. "This has nothing to do with you."

"It has everything to do with me," Snuffy said, growing louder. "You knew it. Tuffy knew it my whole life." He began to shake, his voice growing still louder. "Goofy little brother, can't do a thing. He was right."

"Snuffy, wait," Jack tried to interject, but Snuffy barely heard him.

"He was right, and now I've lost my children. I nearly lost you. I put everyone in danger." Snuffy began screaming uncontrollably. "Everyone here is in danger. Stay clear of Mayor Snuffy—he'll get you killed. Everyone here is in danger."

Tink reached out for him, but Snuffy sprang away.

"He wanted you!" Snuffy shouted at Tinkerbelle. "He wants me hurt, and he'll hurt everyone I love and I won't do a thing about it. I won't do a single thing about it. Everyone here is in danger."

Tink and the crowd stood stunned as they watched Snuffy deteriorate. He was shaking and shouting, literally howling in pain. And then all of a sudden, he went totally still. After a long beat, Snuffy collapsed and silently stared a thousand miles into the space in front of him.

Bertrand and Sarah helped him to a bed in the medical ward. He curled up silently.

Jack and Cookie limped out of the medical ward to meet the folks around town. They both felt a deep responsibility to make things right.

"You set the fire?" Moe the mule wasn't welcoming the dogs, but he'd hear what they had to say.

"No, sir. That was someone else. We laid a spring trap on the path."

"And you knew these dogs before the rains came?" Moe was shooting his best dirty look.

"Yes, sir. We knew all the dogs from the neighborhood. We feel terrible about having anything to do with this."

"I hope to think," Moe said sharply. "How do you do such a thing to folks you know?"

Cookie told how they'd gotten involved, with an emphasis on how slippery and deceitful Tuffy could be. They told how reasonable Tuffy could make it sound if you were willing to be fooled. They told how they got caught up in the sailing, and the recon, and how it came to seem like a game.

Moe lit on the sailing part and how the floaters were crafted. He called his boys out to hear all about the sailing machines. After much explanation and another hundred apologies, the dogs were led by Moe and the boys on a little scavenger hunt of their own.

CHAPTER THIRTEEN

The Other Side

By the grace of whatever is holy for two brothers in a fake boat lost in the middle of an ocean born of biblical rains, the boys found the other side. They simply continued following the vague directions of the songbirds and doing with the wind and sails what they'd been doing, and there they were.

Artie took the sail away from the wind to slow down as they approached the steep climb of a grassy hill. When the floater coasted into arm's reach, he took the ribbon attached to the front and hopped over the side. He sank like a rock.

Moose listened to the mysterious quiet and realized they weren't getting any closer to the hill. As he peered over the bow, Artie burst out of the water with an enormous gasp. His tight grip on the ribbon was his only salvation as the hill on which they were trying to land fell straight down into the water. It might have been a hundred feet deep where they sat.

"Help!" Artemis cried between gasps. "Moosie, help me back in the boat!"

Moose scrambled for the other end of the ribbon. He took a firm hold and pulled with all his strength.

Artemis bobbed up again, shouting, "Moose! Too deep, can't reach." He bobbed up and down again. "Can't reach. Can't swim. Moose!"

Moose wasn't frightened. He took the ribbon and gave it a wrap around the back of each paw for a sure grip, something he'd seen the builder crews do back home. He braced himself against the side and tugged with all his might. He tumbled backward.

Moose smiled at his own power, impressed that he could yank his sizable brother to safety with one giant pull. He hadn't known it was possible. Then the end of the ribbon smacked him wet in the face. Moose screamed. He'd just separated Artemis from his lifeline.

When Moose hit the water, he wasn't entirely sure if he could swim either. Both animals had spent time playing in the stream and the lake, but ordinarily the water was shallow enough to walk around. Moose couldn't remember if he'd ever been in over his head, which he was right now in every way he could be.

The water was cold and dark. Moose looked furiously for Artemis and instinctively kicked his legs to dive lower.

Time was moving slowly, and although he was panicked, there was a calmness around him and a lot of time before he needed to breathe. He spotted Artemis, sinking quickly, moving farther and farther from him. Then something strange happened. Moose dove like a frogman, fast and deep, and circled underneath the big porker. With the strength of Superman, he tugboated his hefty brother to the surface.

Artemis's head burst above the water with a gargantuan gasp, and then he immediately began sinking again. Moose gulped air, then calmly hooked a haunch under his brother's left tusk and backstroked them both to the steep shore of grass. With a kick and a lunge beyond his wildest imagination, he pushed his brother sideways to a narrow stretch of dry land. Then he climbed up after him.

They lay still for a minute, catching their breath. Artemis was staring at Moose as if to say, "What have you done with my little brother?"

Moose rolled toward his big bro with a childlike gentleness. "Are you okay?"

Artemis saw only his baby brother and was confused. He nodded, but they didn't speak for a long time.

Artemis and Moose climbed to a high plateau on the steep hillside. Artie rummaged around the sparse shrubbery and produced some berries. He was fatigued and couldn't shake the horror of his near-death plunge. They sat quietly eating while Artie kept testing a way to broach the subject of how his little brother had saved his life.

Moose had given it less thought than he had before he jumped in the water. Something had stirred inside him, and he just operated on automatic.

A few berries later, Artemis said, "So, you know, uh . . .thanks, Moosie, thanks for jumping in after me."

"Were you scared?" Moose asked gently.

"Sure I was scared." Artemis chuckled self-consciously. "I never thought a shoreline could be so deep. I sank like a bag of hammers."

They sat in quiet contemplation until Moose remembered. "I didn't know I could swim either. I guess I can."

"Sure you can. You swim like a fish." Artemis slid over to tussle his brother's hair. "I was a goner, little dude, and you jumped in and saved me like a big dolphin or something."

They roughhoused playfully, and Moose began to giggle.

"How'd you learn to do that?" Artie asked as he tusk-tossed the little guy onto his back.

It was a maneuver they'd practiced a thousand times, and Moose had gotten good at landing in a riding mount on his brother. From there he could get a paw full of mane hair and kick and holler like a rodeo rider. Artemis snorted and bucked, and the two laughed and rolled in the grass. That little bit of horseplay broke the tension, and a small bellyful of berries was enough to nod the boys off for a while.

Snuffy was still laid up in the medical tent. He hadn't spoken at all since he'd collapsed. Tink and Sarah were tending to him, but there was little anyone could do.

"Snuffy spent his whole life bullied by that monster of a big brother," Tinkerbelle said.

She lay her head across Snuffy's neck to get him to stir, but he remained motionless.

"The brother won't harm your children," Sarah consoled Tinkerbelle. "There's no bad blood between them. Molly's his niece."

Sarah gently scratched Tink on her shoulders. Pandora joined them quietly. Tinkerbelle was glad for the support. The women of Pugville were there for each other. It was a source of great strength.

"These boys have been at each other forever." Tinkerbelle sighed. "It's never going to change."

"Your children are strong," Pandora said. "They're smart and extremely capable. You have to remember that."

"They're babies," Tinkerbelle said, almost teary but too exhausted to cry.

"Artie's no baby," Sarah said authoritatively. "Moosie is fine, and they'll find their sister. You can be sure of that."

"Artie's a big strong man," Pandora added for emphasis.

"Everybody's a big strong man until he isn't," Tinkerbelle said, staring at Snuffy. "You're big and strong. She's big and strong. In the end, where does it get you?"

"We take what we get, and we make it better," Sarah philosophized. "You of all people know that. We work and we fight, and we make things better for everyone."

"As if we ever get any credit," Pandora spat reflexively, and for the first time in a long while, the women shared a hearty laugh.

Artie and Moose awoke when the shade they'd fallen asleep under gave way to bright sunshine. The nap was rejuvenating. They gathered up the last berries and started up the hill again. Near the crest line, they were greeted by a lone goat.

"Maaahhhhning," the young kid bayed.

This made his partner laugh and give away his hiding place behind a big tree. He stepped forward.

"Nah, we don't talk like that," the first said.

"That's sheep," the second declared. "We ain't no sheep."

"Good morning to you," Artemis said pleasantly.

The first goat stepped closer—a little *too* close—and said, "We don't get much company up here. You two lost or something?"

"Yeah, or something," the second kid repeated as a sign of intimidation.

"We were just walking over the hill," Artemis said, taking a small step backward.

The goat stepped into the space Artie had just created and said, "You know, we ain't got no extra grain for a pig like you."

"Or your fluffy little girlfriend," added the other, and they both laughed.

Artemis lost any doubt the two were spoiling for a fight. He tried his best to keep a calm demeanor as he took another step backward. "Look, fellas, all we're doing is walking over this hill. We're not looking for any trouble."

"Trouble?" The first kid turned toward his friend. "I didn't say anything about trouble. Did you say anything about trouble?"

"Not me," he said. "The only one talking 'bout trouble is pig-boy here."

Artemis backed up until he was in front of Moose. He gathered the pug behind him and continued backing away from the two punks. "This is all a big misunderstanding. We're sorry we bothered you. We'll just be on our way . . ."

"Which way would that be, exactly?" The voice was so deep it was booming, and it was directly behind the boys.

They turned quickly to see a giant ram with huge curled horns towering over them. Moose shot away and cowered behind the nearest tree.

Artemis stood wide-eyed. Slowly, and without moving his head, he walked his hindquarters around behind him.

He stood squared up to the enormous beast. "We're just walking, sir, that's all," Artemis said slowly.

"Well, you won't be walking for long," the huge ram shouted, breaking into an evil laugh as he scraped his hooves in the dirt.

Artemis lowered his center of gravity and braced for the worst head butt ever. The ram focused his aim and readied for attack.

Then, in a blur of motion, Moose came flying at the beast, feetfirst, and landed a ninja-style kick to its lips. The ram's jaw went up, and his horn went down. Moose grabbed the horn, twisting the giant sheep even farther out of order, and flung himself onto Artie's back. Moose grabbed a hunk of mane and clung to his brother for dear life. Artemis lunged for the ram's knees, head down, tusks up, and burrowed into the monster. A roar of pain rattled the day as the giant animal tumbled into a defeated heap. Artemis and Moose barely escaped being crushed by the falling behemoth.

Artie spun on his hooves to face the two punk goats, Moose astride his back like a gunslinger. "We'll just be on our way now, unless there's something else?" Artemis was snorting and scraping like a giant bull, looking the first one dead in the eyes.

The goats froze for one long beat, then vanished in opposite directions like cartoon cats.

Artemis galloped over the crest of the hill with Moose shouting behind them, "Moose and Artie! Artimooose!"

Artemis had to laugh as he carried his little brother as fast as he could go.

Molly tried not to show how frightened and uncomfortable she was inside Tuffy's ghastly house. Her Pugville home was small and warm, built into a grand sycamore. It had dirt floors and was filled with the constant fragrance of fresh air. This place smelled of mildew and barnyard, rot and despair. She could feel the hum of fear and uncertainty.

The lower-level den was the heartbeat of Tuffy's operation. There were many storage areas filled with salvage that Tuffy called inventory, and there were several workstations for small repairs and reclamations. Clothing and jewelry and smaller housewares were inside, and larger projects such as wood, metal pieces, furniture, and large housewares were finished and stored in the garage.

Parades of vermin constantly carried and moved items scavenged throughout the broken neighborhood, and insects by the thousands moved in clouds to their tasks. It made Molly want to barf. She saw sloppy dogs and ugly warthogs everywhere. The dogs were all lazy and disinterested, and the hogs made Molly miss her brother Artemis all the more. One hog kept close to Tuffy, and seeing them together gave her chills. It was like looking right at Snuffy and Artie. Molly wondered if she'd ever see them again. It made her so homesick she always cried.

Artemis ran like the wind for as long as he could, until his adrenaline started to level off. The crest of the hill flattened off into a clearing inside a thick tree line. He headed for the trees to find a safe resting place. The near-death experience had pumped him up, and the bizarre fight had his mind racing faster than his feet. He slowed to a trot and surveyed their surroundings. Artemis ducked in at a patch of grass and decided it was a fine place to rest.

Moose had dismounted and was walking a circle around the soft grass for a place to land. "That was terrific," he said as he lay his belly flat in the cool moss. "You really crumbled that giant. *Pow!* Right in the knees."

Artemis stepped behind the boy to view the clearing. "Yeah, yeah, that was a lucky break," he said. "How did you hit that monster?"

"I dunno. I just jumped, I guess . . ."

Artie took a long look at the pug. "Nice jump, kid."

Moose sighed mightily, and his eyelids grew heavy.

Artemis stood still for a long beat, then dove at the little guy. Moose didn't move a muscle, and Artie nearly broke his neck trying not to crush him. "Awright!" Artemis shouted, "What's the deal with you?"

"I don't know." Moose shrugged, wide-eyed and innocent.

Artemis swung around to Moose's side. "Tell me everything."

"When I was hiding behind that tree, I couldn't move," Moose began. "I was so scared. Then I felt rumbly in my belly and my eyes went dark, I guess. And then I couldn't see much. I could only feel myself moving. I don't know."

"You couldn't see?"

"Not really. I could see you underwater, but I don't remember how we got to the shore."

Artie gave him the Bertrand stare. "So you're just a little freak, is that it?"

Moose looked up at his big brother with wide eyes. "I don't know that either. What's a freak?"

The boys continued close to the tree line for cover. Artie insisted they walk apart so they could keep better watch over one another. He made Moose promise to hide if there was more trouble. Once in a while Artie would sneak up on the little guy in a fake attack, to test his magical fighting reflexes. Moose responded like a goofy little brother with no skills at all. So far, he'd shown no further sign of his inner ninja warrior.

The sun was falling low, so they searched for a safe place to camp overnight.

"It should be surrounded on three sides, and have some vegetation for cover," Artie coached his little brother. "And we should start gathering food."

Moose couldn't believe his own brother's intelligence. They dove into the brush, looking for a suitable spot and some plants that looked edible. As far as food was concerned, they had an excellent education to draw from. Uncle Bertrand had seen to it. Artie also knew they should skip building a fire. The moon would be out, and having a fire announce their location was a poor idea. Given what they'd gone through, it was best if they stayed hidden—and quiet. They teased each other about snoring, each brother swearing the other was a liar.

The boys foraged some berries and succulent vines and dug in under an accommodating philodendron. The sun set, and the boys huddled together for warmth. The giant hanging leaf they camped under helped retain their body heat, and it was a relatively pleasant night.

As darkness surrounded them, their thoughts turned to their family. They wondered about their parents' reaction to their departure. They took turns imagining the scene, and with each telling, they imagined even more trouble. The night of horror stories kept their minds off how crazy they were to be so exposed, so unprepared, and so uncertain of what to do next.

Molly was the guest of honor at dinner. The meal had been planned with a different tone because it was intended for Tinkerbelle, but Tuffy used the opportunity to intimidate the youngster and let her know her place. He helped her to the seat of honor, right next to Crock. Tuffy's meanest and ugliest were all in attendance.

Tuffy made introductions. "This here is Uncle Snake, and this is Mr. Roach, who, along with Rat, will be around anytime you need anything."

Molly swallowed hard and lost her sarcastic fire. If hell had a waiting room, she was in it.

"Good, then," Tuffy said. "Let's eat."

Molly was forcing down some ghastly bean concoction when Roach jumped on the side of her plate to say hello. It crossed her mind to slurp him up, or maybe just smash him, but she wasn't entirely comfortable testing Tuffy's tolerance for violence. She just stared at him in horror as she lost the last of her appetite.

"Everyone here works." Roach was trying to be helpful, but his voice had a sinister tone as he introduced Molly to the inventory supervisor for people clothes. "This is Mrs. S. She'll supervise your first job, sorting clothing. You start tomorrow morning . . . Enjoy."

Mrs. S was a salamander, or some kind of ancient reptile. She had a horrible demeanor and a raspy voice. "Don't bother learning a lot of names, honey," she told Molly. "You won't be around too long. They never are."

Molly felt disgusted as the salamander cackled until she coughed. The little pug was frightened and very near tears.

CHAPTER FOURTEEN

Minor Key

The boys woke with the sun, shaking and stretching. They gobbled the last of the food as Artemis scratched up some dirt and plotted their destination like a sandlot football play.

Moose concurred it was an excellent plan and excused himself for nature's call. He wandered deeper into the clump of trees and sniffed out a suitable place to do his business. When he popped back into a clearing, he could see Artemis walking away.

"Hey," Moose shouted as he approached. "Just where ya think yer goin' to, ya big mule?"

The hog stopped dead at the sound of his voice. Moose broke into a trot to catch up and gave him a playful rump bump, which made him giggle. The hog slowly turned and grabbed the little dog by the nape of his neck. He lifted Moose off the ground and held him in front of his face.

Then they both froze, eyes wide. Moose hadn't caught Artie, but some strange hog who looked just like him.

"And just who might you be?" the scowling hog demanded.

They both continued to stare. Moose couldn't believe how much this hog looked like Artie. The animal let out a piercing whistle, and several more razorbacks surrounded them.

"Hey, Buster, whatcha got there?"

"Tell me this isn't a teeny version of that dog down the hill."

Buster passed the pug to his cousin Clete, who gave him a thorough eyeballing. Clay stared over his shoulder.

"I'm thinking ransom," Buster plotted out loud. "I'm thinking we can get whatever we want for a little dog that's just like Tuffy."

Clete and Clay couldn't disagree. This pup surely had some connection to Tuffy, and that was bargaining power. This was definitely something to take to Anarkey.

Artemis heard the whistle and stealthily searched from the tree line, finally spotting the hogs and Moose a hundred yards off or more. The three hogs handling Moose were as big as him, at least, and there were more. He followed them, frantically searching for a viable ambush.

Artemis was sick with worry about his little brother. But considering what he'd seen from Moose the day before, he told himself that he might just as well be worried for the health of the other hogs. Artemis smiled to think how Moose would soon snap into another ninja trance and make pork chops. Artemis whispered under his breath a message for the universe to carry: "Stay calm, little guy. I'm coming to get you."

The hogs reached the outlook platform with Moose in tow. The place was virtually covered by the great weeping willow. They stood outside the shelter and called inside. "Key! I know you can hear me, Key. I got sumthin' that'll interest you. Do you hear, boy?"

"Buster, what have you got yourself up to now?" Key asked, poking his head outside.

"Only the ticket to our rich and beautiful future."

That was enough to give the cousins a laugh. Key hooked a tusk and dragged Buster inside. The crew poked the pug inside and followed closely.

Inside, Key took a long look at Moose. Something was wrong, but he couldn't decide what. He told the rest of the cousins to get lost, and they scattered. Key continued to study the pug for a long time. There was no denying the little guy looked exactly like a young Tuffy. It was the large black eyes against the fawn color of the boy's face that was the best match. Add some gray around the boy's flat, wet nose and you could tell they were family. It almost made

Tuffy seem like he could have been young and innocent at some time in his miserable life.

"That's what I thought," Buster said, taking credit for a thing that was actually way over his head.

"So what do you think it means?" Key asked.

"I think Tuffy'll be interested in trading for one of his kind."

"Where'd he come from?" Key asked.

"Well, he kinda come outta nowhere," Buster said. "See, I was digging fer some seeds up in the flats, and alla sudden here, this one comes hollerin' and gives me a slap on the behind. That's when I grabbed him up."

"Out of nowhere?" Key was incredulous.

"Out from the trees behind the flats," Buster corrected himself. "Don't know why he was tryin' to catch me. Lost maybe."

Key stopped him and pulled him close. "You think this is just some random dog?" Key was trying to sort it all out in his head while taking advantage of the opportunity to poke at Buster some more. "You don't think it's too much like Tuffy?"

"They all look the same," the hog argued. "Geez, look at us."

"Exactly," Key said, already thinking on the next level. "We look alike but not all the same. Something ain't right here." Anarkey needed time to think this through. It was an opportunity for sure, but one that could turn out badly if he wasn't careful. The first thing to do was limit his exposure. "Leave the dog here," he instructed Buster. "Then gather at the shack behind Anderson Ranch. Sit tight and wait for me." Key emphasized the last bit of instruction so he knew Buster wouldn't try to think for himself.

Artemis followed the hogs to what looked like the crest of the hill, where they all disappeared into the brush. The Anderson Ranch had been the largest and most renowned property in the hills. It, too, had been ruined by the storms, save for a wooden shack settled under a clump of trees. It was a tackle shack, used to service the barns and nearby exercise track, all of which had blown away in the tempest.

Artie made it to the shack just as the hogs made it to the observation deck. It seemed like the perfect hiding place. Artie ducked inside and peered through the damaged wall. He watched silently until finally, the hogs poked through the willow tree and headed toward him. He tried not to panic. There was some distance between them, and they could be headed anywhere. But they kept heading toward him. As they grew dangerously near, Buster hollered for Clay and crossed toward him. Artie held his breath to listen to their conversation.

Some of the same signal whistles sounded, and the razorback crew began to assemble at the shack. Artemis scanned the interior, looking for another exit, but there was only one door. He could see through most of the interior walls to the outside, so badly was the place damaged, but there wasn't a spot wide enough for his frame to squeeze through. He was trapped.

Artemis heard the hogs growing even closer. He heard Buster repeat the instruction to lay low in the shack. Artemis dug into the corner, waiting to be found.

Going anywhere blindly put Tuffy in a foul humor. Anarkey met him halfway up the hill to soften the mood. He hoped Tuffy would reward his kindness.

Together they walked inside the observation deck to find Moose. There was no mistake. It was like looking right into Snuffy's face.

Tuffy took a seat and said nothing for the longest time.

Rarely was Anarkey more nervous than when Tuffy said nothing for a long time.

"The pup is definitely family," Tuffy finally said. "This is truly a great day." Tuffy embraced the hog and thanked him profusely for bringing such good fortune. "Of all the great things you've done, my boy, this is the best."

Anarkey grew excited at the possibilities that would be coming to his crew. Tuffy's head was filled with the prospect of having a brand new pug to train in his image.

"Your family has been a wonderful addition to me and my operation, and now you've found me a genuine heir," Tuffy said, then paused meaningfully. "You understand this means I no longer have use for your services." His words rang with the sincere gratitude that comes from a truly evil mind. "You and your kin are excused, effective immediately. Thanks for everything."

With that, he took the pup and left.

Artemis was still backed against the wall of the tackle shack when Key arrived. The young hog had a few scrapes and cuts from a brief escape attempt. He'd been no match for this crew of outlaws, but he'd tried just the same. That gave him some credibility with the family.

Clay was just outside the shack, briefing Key. "That's how we found him," Clay said. "He was in the wrong place at the wrong time."

Key was taking it all in, deep in thought, peeking at the young hog through the broken wall. "Right time," he responded reflexively.

Clay furrowed his brow and questioned Key with a lost look.

"Wrong place, right time." Key sighed heavily. "If you're in the wrong place but it's the wrong time, nothing happens."

Clay nodded blankly.

Key leaned into his cousin and whispered, "It has to be the right time."

Clay remained confused as Anarkey walked away.

"Okay, so the little dog is your brother," Anarkey said sarcastically. "There's a goat down the road . . . is she yer mom?"

His joke raised a conspiratorial snigger and broke the tension in the room. Key was showing off a little, glad for the distraction. He hadn't told his family that Tuffy had kicked all of them to the curb, and right now he didn't have to worry how they'd take the news.

"Look, pal," Artemis chided, "my mom was a pig, and I was raised in a family of dogs. What's your excuse, ya mutt?"

Key was impressed. The little guy had courage, if not sense. "You do realize you're tied to a wall, don't you?" Key asked threateningly.

"So untie me," Artie suggested, "and you and me can have a go."

The threat drew jeers from the peanut gallery. Key gave the boy a firm smack to the chops, but Artemis stuck to his story.

He continued to say that he and the pug were brothers, and Molly was their sister. "The only reason I'm here," Artie insisted, "is to get the two of them home safe. I didn't know about you all, and I don't want to know about you all. You'll never see us again."

Buster finally lost his cool completely. "I'm tired of this!" he shouted, running a vicious head butt to the ribs of the prisoner. The hard smack left Artie coughing and wheezing.

Key hooked Buster and tossed him toward the door in a seething rage. Clete stepped between the two just in time. Clete cooled Key with a look, and then gored the young cousin outside. The rest of the crew went to assess the damage to Artie's side.

"Get off him!" Key bellowed, and the crew stood down. "I've had enough of this."

He started to unstrap the hog from the wall. Reaching under, toward Artie's right forelock, Key stopped cold and stared for a long time. Then he ripped Artie down, wall and all, and flung him to the ground outside. *"Pin him down!"*

The crew took the boy from all limbs on his back. Key whispered to Clete, who turned slowly toward Artie with a look of astonishment. Both hogs closed in on Artemis. They roughly spread his haunches so wide it shot a hot pain through the boy's entire frame.

They were staring at a bluish-green mark that looked like a blurry star. It had to be a bruise, Key thought. The only other thing like it that he'd ever seen was in the very same place on his very own leg.

The cousins lingered a long time inspecting, then backed off, looking at one another in disbelief. Both slowly turned their eyes toward Artie.

"What?" Artemis shot back angrily. "What?"

The star on Artie was a birthmark, and it nearly perfectly matched Anarkey's. The math was undeniable. The birthmark was undeniable. Anarkey had a son. Key remembered every minute he ever spent with Mercy, every minute he spent searching for her. He was relieved and angry and saddened to finally learn her fate. He was indescribably happy to learn he had a son. The mixture of all these feelings was about to break him in two. He couldn't stop grabbing Artie and looking deeply into his face, every time seeing a different part of his wonderful Mercy.

They talked a long time about Snuffy and Tinkerbelle, about Moose and Molly, about the ducks and the mules and the lake in the valley. It made Artie feel a great deal better describing his home. It made him feel grounded, like he had a place where he belonged.

"Mercy would be so happy to hear all this," Key kept saying. "She dreamed of that kind of life."

Then Artie told of the horrific events in Pugville, the fire and the kidnapping, and then coming across the water.

Key smelt the burning stench of Tuffy and Thugville all over the report. And he began to feel a steely resolve. These were things about which Key knew a thing or two.

"We're back together," Anarkey said, addressing the entire family in the clearing outside the shed. "We are at full strength. Plus, we have this young hog here, who is my son."

The family cheered.

"We also have a new plan. Nobody works in Tuffy's town anymore, and that was his choice. So we're just gonna have to rob the old fart."

The words elicited the biggest cheer of all. The hogs spent the day plotting and scheming at the old pug's expense. Artie listened carefully for his best chance to find and free his brother and sister.

CHAPTER FIFTEEN

Reunion

Molly awoke with newfound optimism. Ever since she'd been torn from her home, she'd felt a nagging sense of dread, but not today. Today she felt overwhelmingly that something good was about to happen. Molly spent most nights trying to concentrate on her family, hoping that holding them in her mind would help them find her. She tried to reach her brothers through the cosmos. She tried to guide Artemis to her so she could watch him tear apart this awful place.

Rat came to escort her to the den as he did every morning. When they met Roach in the hallway, Molly nodded and smiled

Roach stepped aside with a pleasant, "Good morning."

When Rat stepped ahead to clear the hall, Molly, as casually as possible, bent down and slurped up the tiny bug in her mouth. *This is going to be a good day,* she thought.

Molly could hear his muffled screams as she rolled the insect around her palette like she was tasting a fine wine. Then she spat him hard to the floor.

"Hey! What the . . . *hey*!" was all Roach could manage as he checked for all his limbs.

Molly leaned in for a sniffing.

"Hey!" Roach shouted again as he pressed himself against the wall, searching for an escape.

Rat finally noticed the pair. "Hey!" he shouted. "Wait. Don't. You can't eat Roach."

"I wouldn't eat him," Molly replied casually. "He tastes like dirt." Then she leaned down to give Rat a long lick across the length of his body. Rat ran screaming down the hallway, over Roach's stern objection.

"Eww!" Molly shouted as Rat scurried out of sight. "You taste like a hog fart. And I know some hog fart."

Left alone in a dark hallway with a crazed teenage pug, Roach tried to assert himself. Still spitting out dog slobber, he insisted, "Now, young lady, you listen to me . . ."

Molly reached out with a swipe of her tongue and gobbled him back inside. She giggled at how he continued his muffled exhortations even as he was about to be crunched.

As she turned to head down the hallway, she walked smack into Crock, with Rat cowering behind him. The giant reptile was bent at the waist and holding out a paw, as though Molly had been caught chewing gum in class. Molly tilted her head and widened her eyes at the old dinosaur.

Then Molly caught a familiar whiff. Her ears perked up, and her hair stood on end. It was Moose for sure, but it couldn't be. She quickly spat out the bug and sneezed to clear her senses. There it was again, the unmistakable scent of her brother.

Molly scratched like a speeding race car down the hallway toward the smell.

"Moosie!" Molly followed her nose to the most beautiful sight in her young life.

"Molly!" Moose yelped, flinging himself on his sister.

The two tumbled together in a mad embrace of sniffing and pawing, leaping and crying.

"These pups are my family," Tuffy proclaimed to everyone. "Spread the word. You will treat them as you would me. They both live here now."

Tuffy ordered that the living quarters be refashioned as in the old days, each child to a separate room, and then remain completely off-limits to crew. He ordered the finest adornments be selected from inventory and lavished on the children. "They'll work for their keep, though," he said as he huddled with his top lieutenants. "Put the girl in charge of inventory," he continued, "and the boy will learn every phase of this operation. Start him in the shop. Keep them supervised at work and otherwise locked in their rooms."

Tuffy's lieutenants began hustling to Tuffy's orders when he called them back. "Also, I've informed Anarkey that he and his hogs will no longer be needed. Keep a good watch out for them." Tuffy shot a laser stink eye to Snake. "And keep these kids safe."

Tuffy gave the children jobs in his family factory. He would teach them about work and responsibility with a stern hand, and then favor them to build loyalty. His long, badgering speeches about discipline and fortitude were always compensated with gifts and recreation. Tuffy believed fear was the same as love. He regaled them with stories of how everything had improved around the neighborhood since their parents' time. He assured them in the most sinister way that Snuffy and Tinkerbelle would be across the water soon, that they'd all be together as a family. The children wanted very much to believe him.

Moose worked brutal hours in the workshop under intimidating supervision. He liked cobbling broken pieces into new inventions, but was always too scared to enjoy the work. He got locked in his room at night, which made him lonely and even more frightened. Tuffy ordered him along to witness a beating from time to time, when Snake had to remind an ambitious worker who was boss. It was always a grotesque and menacing event that made him sad and queasy. Tuffy and Snake would afterwards feed him some nonsense about justice and how people learn.

Molly's time was no better at Mrs. S's inventory post. Nobody talked about what had become of Mrs. S, and Molly never asked. She was also locked away at night, and she talked to her brother through the doors and across the hall. They talked about how soon their parents would come, but they really didn't beleive it. They were trying to make each other feel better about missing home so terribly. They also tried to make each other laugh at the bizarre creatures they met in their new surroundings. It got less funny every day.

CHAPTER SIXTEEN

Revenge

Jack and Cookie never returned from Pugville. The sailing crews buried two oars in the sand by the Thugville sign as an unmarked monument to them. The sailing rigs that made it home weren't retired, but kept close at hand. The beach by the jungle had become something of a commercial marina where various activities shoved off.

Bones and Earl kept *The Swift* running for sightseeing and recreation. Luke and Otter named the other boat *The Villians,* a purposeful misspelling to indicate living in Thugville and being cool like an outlaw. Most of the sailing and building crews helped with the operation, and dressed the boats with cushions and coolers, tackle and equipment, all procured through Tuffy. Seeing the immediate popularity, Tuffy took credit for the idea.

Key and Artie navigated a back road out of the hills to the shore of the jungle. They organized a fishing trip with

Bones and Earl, and the four of them went out on the water right away. Bones and Earl had never seen a fish caught, but they took the charter with gusto.

"Can't guarantee you're gonna catch anything, but we can take you out," Bones explained preemptively.

"We understand how fishing works," Key said cheerfully. "You get us out there, and we'll take our chances."

Anarkey directed Bones around to the north and out of sight. Earl was busy untangling fishing lines when the hogs told him to set the gear aside. They told Bones to stop the boat.

"Whoa, boys," Bones said, immediately suspicious. "We don't want no trouble."

Anarkey moved close to the ferret. "We don't want to fish," he said in a sinister tone. "We just want to talk." Anarkey explained how his long-lost son had arrived, and the purpose of their visit became clear.

Bones and Earl stammered about how they'd only been doing what they were told, and how they'd had no choice.

"Do you think you have a choice now?" Artemis piped up.

"Hey!" Bones raised his hands and backed up a step. "What kind of talk is that?"

"You kidnapped my sister," Artie said, taking a step closer. "It's that kind of talk."

Bones and Earl got to talking. Fast. They told how it all came to be, how it was supposed to be a practical joke, how they'd be dead already if they'd hurt the girl.

"So you'll help us get her back?" Artemis asked.

"If I say no, do I have to learn to swim?" Bones asked.

"Nope," Key said convincingly. "We just wanted to know how much love you guys have for Tuffy, and if there's a possibility you'd be willing to move against him."

Bones laughed out loud. "Are you kidding? The whole town would be willing to move against him."

Mole had developed an efficient method for cleaning out a block of houses. Instead of working one house at a time, he surveyed the next home ahead of his crew to design and prioritize the work. This let him focus on several places at once. Mole had learned that every house was in a different state of disrepair, with different levels of inventory.

Mole entered through the front of a single-story home that was set back from the street behind a yard filled with mud and fallen trees. A house like this always held less value, but made for less work. When he pushed through the door, he took a moment to survey the cramped space.

"Might be less than you expected inside this one."

Mole recognized the hog's voice and froze in fear of another awful beating.

"Don't be scared," Buster said from inside the darkness. "If we were here to hurt you, we'd have done it already."

Mole wasn't exactly calmed. "So what do you want then?" he asked, still bracing for a whooping.

"We came to talk a little business," Clete said from the other side of Mole.

Mole jumped two feet.

"Easy, son," Clete said in a calm and friendly voice. "Best you just hear us out."

The three took a seat in what had once been a family room.

"You know we already emptied a house or two down this street here," Clete began. "You know you're gonna have to report that to Tuffy sooner or later."

"I suspected," Mole said frankly. "You guys do sloppy work."

Clete chuckled. "We sure do, by golly. We sure do make a mess of things when we don't care much about getting caught."

"So what's that to me?" Mole wasn't sure if the hogs were playing some sick game before they beat him up anyway.

"What's that to you is this: How many times you think that dog is gonna let you go on getting robbed?" Buster phrased his words like a question, but they were clearly a threat.

"Because," Clete continued, "we mean to keep robbing the dog. And we don't see no reason you should get fed to an alligator because of it."

That threat stung. Mole knew they were right, that Tuffy valued his property much more than he valued his men.

"We're gonna take Tuffy's town," Clete said plainly. "You'll want to be on our side when we do."

The words hung in the air for an impossibly long moment.

Mole took a long look in Buster's eyes, and then he turned to face Clete and said clearly and calmly, "I'm listening."

The hog family knew a hundred paths through the hills and into all parts of the neighborhood. This had been their turf for generations. Word quietly spread of how to find an impossibly well-hidden clearing at the jungle. A small fire was lit at this clearing just after dark, and a fine representation of Thugville gathered around.

"You all know me," Anarkey said, addressing the assembly. "And you all know that my people have been kicked out of town by your leader. What you probably don't know is why." He motioned for Artie to stand beside him. "This is Artemis. We met this week. He's my son."

The clearing grew even quieter.

"He was raised by a family of pug dogs that ran from this place at the start of the great disaster." Anarkey paused dramatically. "I'm sorry, that ain't exactly true. He was raised by part of a pug family. That's right, our friend Tuffy has family across the water that survived."

The crowd began to murmur. The rumors of Pugville were true.

"As you know, Tuffy has a good and sentimental heart, so when he learned about his lost family, and their children—his kin—he did what we all would do. He burned their town and beat their friends, and kidnapped their baby."

The murmurs turned to a ruckus as everyone discussed which parts of the story they'd already known, and more importantly, which parts they hadn't.

Bones and Earl were there with most of the sailing crews, and Bones stood to speak. "I captured that girl myself," he said. "And not a day goes by where I'm not sick about the whole thing." Bones delved into the story of the attack and how Tuffy had convinced them to participate. He shared Tuffy's assurances, and the depths of the pug's deceit and trickery.

Mole and his crew also shared stories of Tuffy's violence and double-dealing. Mole told how Tuffy and Snake made him toss a beating to one of his own, an act for which he'd never forgive himself.

Key's plan was an easy sell. Everyone in the town had a story about being bested by the ultimate con man.

"My family has been working these parts for generations," Anarkey began again. "We take what we need, and we use what we take. We're no angels, but those who came before us gave us a code, and we honor it. When you ride with us, everybody's equal, everybody gets."

A torrent of testimonials about Tuffy's greed and intimidation poured forth. Clete and Clay began collecting specifics about the compound and Tuffy's habits. They made a list of who would stand by Tuffy, and their weaknesses. Artie and Buster mostly listened, newfound cousins impatient for a fight. The rest of the hogs and their new confederates shared critical intelligence and made enormous progress throughout the night.

CHAPTER SEVENTEEN

Showdown

It had been days since Snuffy had spoken, since he'd been placed in the bed in the medical unit. All the folks in Pugville had cleaned the mess, and life was returning to normal, but Sarah and Tinkerbelle continued to stand helplessly over the wounded soul.

"We have to get him up," Sarah said. "I don't care if he's not talking. He has to move around."

"Will it hurt him?" Tinkerbelle was overwrought.

"I've checked him in every way I know," Sarah said, furrowing her brow. "There's nothing physically wrong with him."

"Poor, sweet pug," Tink lamented. "He's just checked out?"

"He's just checked out."

Tinkerbelle sobbed quietly just staring at her broken man. Her missing children were tearing a hole in her heart, and the only thing she had left was lost in another world. She was simply numb with sadness and she couldn't imagine how she could carry on.

Bertrand happened by to check on them. "Any change?"

"He hasn't moved or spoken," Sarah said, giving the old man a soft caress. "I say we get him up."

"Then up he shall get," Bertrand said joyfully. "Come on, my friend, wakey, wakey."

Bertrand reached a scaly arm under the pug and sat him on his haunches. Snuffy molded into position without responding. Bertrand nodded to Sarah, and the two lifted the dog off the bed onto the soft grass below.

"Come, my friend, there's something you absolutely must see," Bertrand said in a lilting voice, and the three managed to get Snuffy across the square toward the water.

The sun was bright and warm on the beach as the friends settled Snuffy's rear into the sand. He sat staring off into nowhere. Bertrand and Sarah propped and tended to him, stuck like a statue on the beach.

"A little sunshine might snap him out of it," Tink said, fighting off her deep despair to try and bring some part of her life back to her. "Snuffy, look, isn't it wonderful?"

"I have a little more sunshine yet," Bertrand said brightly. "A little more sunshine yet."

Just then Moe and his sons dragged three boats along the sand from around the bend. Jack and Cookie were close behind.

"What have you done?" Tinkerbelle gasped.

Bertrand climbed on one and began fussing with the controls. They were worthy craft, solid doors at the bottom and many construction items attached by braided twigs and vines.

"The birds helped a lot," Moe said. "And Jack and Cookie here knew just how to make them."

"Do they float?" Sarah asked.

"Welp," Moe said. "A few of the squirrels took 'em on the water and didn't sink. But I'm not getting on those things." Moe erupted into his infectious cackle.

"Of course they float," Cookie interrupted. "We sailed boats just like this countless times across the water."

From his seat behind the conversation, Snuffy began to stir.

"So, forgive me, but what are they for?" Tinkerbelle was still a little shocked by the bizarre vessels.

"They're for bringing your kids home," Jack said.

Tinkerbelle let out a sob and sank to the ground. She knocked into Snuffy, who rolled limply to his side. Tinkerbelle heard him say, in a tiny whisper, "I have to bring my kids home."

"There's not much to it really," Jack instructed. "You just swing these things this way and that until it works." Jack and Cookie were teaching everyone how to operate the floaters. It was a thing simple to teach, but hard to master.

The three pupils were taking dry runs on the sand before taking a try in the water. They could catch a wind and make the boat slide slightly around in the sand.

"That's it," Jack said excitedly. "That's how it works."

"Yes," Cookie said in a more cautious tone. "That's how it works on land. When you're out there, you get a lot more action than a bit of sliding."

They decided on a few more dry runs before they risked drowning.

Snuffy was awake and talking, but it wouldn't be fair to say he was up and around. He was still lethargic, and still repeating himself. Sometimes he'd focus and sometimes not, and Tink couldn't be sure how much he comprehended at any time.

"Just keep talking to him," Sarah advised. "Keep him engaged, and he'll eventually find his way back."

That would be easy. There was much to engage, much to learn and discuss as the group seriously considered a trip across the water.

Jack and Cookie also were describing the navigation they'd developed to maintain a straight course across the water. "We'll all be together. Don't worry about that. But if something happens, you should know where you're going."

The system was based on the sun's path across the sky, which had everything to do with knowing what time it was when you launched. It wasn't complicated. It was the simplicity that made it sound dangerous.

"That's it?" Bertrand asked incredulously. "That's all you have to go by?

When the boats from Pugville neared the Thugville shore, there was no sign of life. *The Swift* and *The Villians* were secured on the beach, equipment and tackle neatly tucked away. Jack was piloting the lead boat with Tinkerbelle, who was also attending to a half-conscious Snuffy. Cookie sailed the next closest boat with Sheriff Buck at the tiller, and Sarah had the helm of the last boat in concert with Bertrand.

Tinkerbelle's heart jumped upon seeing the jungle. She tried to get Snuffy to recognize the old place, but he stared blankly, giving little sign anything registered. Everyone had hoped the old neighborhood would snap the pug back to reality.

Jack shouted some final instructions about how to land the boats safely, and all three made a fine docking. Jack and Tink helped Snuffy to the sand, and he suddenly became more animated than he'd been in days.

He sniffed around wildly, then trotted up to the grass where he'd spent a young lifetime playing. "Tuffy's in the jungle," he shouted to Tinkerbelle. "He has to be in the jungle."

Tinkerbelle sobbed in delight. "Yes, sweetheart, Tuffy's lost in the jungle. Look, Snuffy, look. We're here. We're here in the jungle."

Snuffy bounded across the grass like a pup, sniffing the ground, then back to the sand, then bursting back again to the grass. He ran zigzag across the lawn, skidded to a stop, and then ran back again. He dug his paws into the dirt at the edge of the grass, sending a plume of earth through his haunches, then buried his nose deep inside the shallow hole. With a snout full of mud, Snuffy sneezed himself flat onto his butt. And then he focused. He saw Tinkerbelle and Buck. He saw the great expanse of water they'd crossed. He saw Bertrand, Jack, and Cookie.

Sarah approached him carefully.

"Hello, Sarah," Snuffy said from his seat on the grass. "It's truly lovely to see you."

Jack and Cookie sniffed around the new marina to try to uncover what had transpired. Their job was to wait with the Pugville floaters like getaway drivers in case of emergency. Snuffy and Tink walked around the park so Snuffy could regain his bearings. The two bears waded in the shallow water as Bertrand took a short, investigatory swim.

The streets of the old neighborhood were humming like the factory town it had become. The place was still in ruins, but it looked remarkably clean and populated. It broke Snuffy's heart to see their warm and wonderful home made so cold and mechanical. The place felt ugly and desperate. Tinkerbelle walked with Sarah and pointed out their old home and how it had changed so dramatically. Bertrand and the sheriff took a path away from the rest as a security measure.

Tink and Snuffy stood for a long moment in front of the old family home. It felt like a dream. Memories of their old lives washed over them. Walking up to the front door seemed like approaching a haunted castle. Snuffy's belly was rumbling like a hot rod. He gave Tinkerbelle a steady stare, then pushed open the door.

Inside, they felt disoriented. The smells of home and family had been replaced by the foulness of junk and creepy beasts. The static and clatter was unsettling. Through the entry hall and into the kitchen, they suddenly found themselves face-to-face with Tuffy. They were lost for words at how he'd aged so poorly in so short a time. He was nearly sympathetic, until he spoke.

"Tinkerbelle!" Tuffy played off his shock at seeing them, "Snuffy! What a lovely surprise!"

"Hello, Tuffy," Snuffy said, everything within him clenching. "Nice to see that you survived."

"Survived very well, thank you," Tuffy snarked at them. "How was your trip?"

Tinkerbelle interrupted through clenched teeth: "Where . . . are . . . my . . . children?" She suddenly caught their scent and tore up the stairs to the bedrooms. She burst the doors open to find them. Cries of joy filled the air as they fell into a frenzied pile of yelping celebration. This continued for some time before Tinkerbelle remembered to stop and properly inspect the children. She sniffed and pawed every inch until she was satisfied no one had broken them and then smothered them again in hugs and kisses. "Moose, where's your brother?"

"He's still up in the hills, I think," Moose said sheepishly. "We got separated. I think it's my fault."

Tinkerbelle hugged the little boy as he told of getting lost while peeing, and then how he'd met another bunch of hogs like Artie. Moose also remembered nearly drowning, and how he and Artie fought a giant ram, but he was sure those stories were best told another time. His mom asked him if he could find the hills again, and Moose said he was pretty sure he could.

The pugs all ran for the door. But at the landing, they were blocked by a giant alligator.

Crock held up his tiny arm to stop them. "I'm sorry," he said in his best mob guy imitation. "Tuffy has asked if you would join him and Mr. Snuffy on the ver-yan-da." Crock had no idea what a veranda was, but he was proud to use the word Tuffy had made him memorize.

Just then a knock came at the door.

"Do excuse me a moment," Crock said, still well in character.

But as he swung open the front door, he was crushed by the tusks of an angry razorback. Crock fell into a heap. Artemis leaped over the fallen soldier into the loving arms of his family.

Tuffy had shown his brother the whole operation of the old house, winding up in the yard where they'd shared so many memories—good and bad. Tuffy's detail of snarling dogs had been stationed there for intimidation.

"So," Tuffy said boastfully, "what do you think of the old place? Nice, right?"

"It's barely recognizable," Snuffy said. "And it smells like monkey butt." He was brimming with anger and frustration. He stepped close and gave Tuffy a quick sniff. "Nope, I'm mistaken. It's you that smells like monkey butt."

"It's good you're finally home," Tuffy smarmily insisted. "We should have a feast. It will be like old times."

"Thanks all the same," Snuffy said. "But we really must be going."

"I simply won't hear of it," Tuffy said, signaling his thugs to block the exit. "You can't go back to that place you call home. It isn't safe, and it isn't wise. Look what I did to you, and I'm family." Tuffy had thought through this speech a thousand times. "You will stay here. This is your home. We are a family. I can provide everything you'll ever need and more."

Snuffy seethed with anger as Tuffy made his proclamation. "We have more kids to collect, thank you," Snuffy said, trying to be the grown-up. "I have responsibilities, so maybe another time? Glad to see you're not dead. Bye now."

Snuffy turned to leave, but Snake had slithered into position high in the trees, and Tuffy's brutes blocked the exit. Tuffy's advantage was secure.

"You're not going anywhere," Tuffy growled menacingly.

Snuffy heaved a slow, heavy sigh. He turned to face his brother. "You were wrong, you know."

Tuffy chuckled. "Wrong about what?"

"About people." Snuffy had been happy to just leave his brother alone, but he decided to tell him a thing or two. "Taking for yourself doesn't make you a hero, and helping others doesn't make you a chump."

"Is that right?" Tuffy asked sarcastically.

"Yes, you self-entitled, tiny, little man. I've been nearly drowned, frozen, eaten by a bear, stranded on an island, and gone catatonic with worry—all about myself. And you know what? None of it matters. Friends matter, family matters, charity matters . . . but you don't know about any of that. You don't have any of that."

"I have friends, and I have great respect," Tuffy said, puffing up. "I'm revered in my community, you little punk."

"You have lackeys and stooges," Snuffy spat back. "You've never had a friend in your sorry life. You've always been a cheat and a thief."

"And you've always been a baby," Tuffy retorted. "Don't you think it's time to grow up?"

"Our people would have been proud of me," Snuffy said, steaming. "And they would have sent you to the pound."

"You live in a fantasy." Tuffy was losing his cool. "You could never look after yourself, just like you can't keep your own family safe."

The dogs moved closer together. Their shouting grew more threatening.

"I should have beat you down a long time ago." Snuffy seethed with anger.

"You and what wolf pack?" Tuffy shouted into his brother's face.

Snuffy took a swipe, and Tuffy fell over ducking the punch, continued to roll, and mule-kicked his little brother. They snarled and growled and crashed into a heap on the ground. Teeth and knees and claws were pounding and tearing each dog to shreds.

In all the fights they'd had growing up, Snuffy had always been confident his brother would stop short of seriously injuring him. This time was different. Tuffy was fighting to kill. Fur was tearing and ears were bleeding, and Snuffy began to feel defeated by mid-battle, the way he always did, the way he always knew he couldn't really beat his big brother.

Once again, Snuffy drifted from consciousness. But this time his fear of his brother and his sense of purpose catapulted him into a ninja trance. He twisted his big brother into a painful wrestling hold he didn't even know how to accomplish. He landed knees and clawed at pressure points he never knew existed. Each time Tuffy moved, Snuffy crawled into superior positions and laid more hurt on his brother. He could hear Tuffy's cries of pain and fear, but he couldn't feel himself moving. He was kicking and butting and slamming the ever-loving snot out of him as though he were a stuffed toy.

Artie and the family slid through the back door to the patio in time to see Bertrand and Buck loping into the yard by the far side of the house. They immediately drew Tuffy's guard dogs in a loud and vicious attack. Buck rose in a furious growl to intimidate the advancing dogs and knocked Bertrand off his feet and right onto his shell. Bertrand spun helplessly.

Then Anarkey and his crew breeched the back fence and stormed the yard like cavalry. Artemis fell in rank with them and gored his way through the snarling dogs to Bertrand.

"Artie!" the old man shouted in celebration. Artie flipped the old man and Bertrand stood and pop-pop-popped himself into a bear. He and Buck joined the fight with Artie and the hogs.

Tuffy's dogs snarled and bit while Anarkey's hogs stomped and gored. The bears punched and grappled, and sometimes just flung the fighting dogs into the shrubbery. The family home was hosting an old-fashioned melee.

Meanwhile, Snuffy had Tuffy pinned on his back, his neck fully exposed. He kept croaking 'uncle' in surrender while Snuffy slowly squeezed the life out of him. Snuffy either couldn't hear or didn't care, because he didn't let up. This was a once-in-a-lifetime beatdown.

Then he heard Bertrand's shout and finally snapped out of it. Everything became instantly and perfectly clear. He was grown and he was worthy. His life had meaning, and his lifelong tormentor had none. Snuffy eased up and let Tuffy breathe and knew that his whole life had changed in those few minutes. He knew Tuffy could never hurt him again.

Snuffy rose off the old pug, and Tuffy lay helpless and beaten before him, an infantile bully finally given a taste of his own medicine. Snuffy had won the brother contest and could see in Tuffy's eyes that he knew it too. Tuffy looked at Snuffy with gratitude for the first time ever. Snuffy savored the moment, then shrugged and punched his brother's lights out.

Snuffy walked slowly to embrace his family, a new man.

The dogs and the hogs continued to fight at the other end of the yard. Rat, who'd successfully hidden from danger, alerted Roach to the emergency and then ran to Tuffy's aid. He brought rags, water, and bandages.

Roach rallied his troops, and suddenly a swarm of flying insects came buzzing into battle. They were stinging and dive-bombing and mounting an impressive offense. They engulfed the two giant bears in a fog. Both bears were completely distracted, ducking and scratching and swinging blindly at the tiny creatures.

"Hang on!" Buck hollered. "I have the perfect solution."

A deep, rumbling sound announced the thickest, foulest, and greasiest bear fart ever ripped. Bertrand's knees buckled at the first wave of it, and it lingered like a lonely friend.

The insects cried in horror as they fled. The sheriff laughed at his own flatulence, and the two got back to fighting the dogs.

Snake slithered to Tuffy's side long after the nick of time.

"Where were you?" the pug demanded.

"I didn't sign up to fight a bear, old man," Snake hissed. "And I don't need your nonsense any longer. See you around." And with that, the snake disappeared.

The hogs beat back the last of the snarling dogs, and the fighting was finished. The evil stench of Buck's secret weapon also was nearly gone. Snuffy and family stood redeemed at one end of the yard, and Tuffy lay at the other. In the middle stood Anarkey and his hogs, with Mole and crew on one flank and the sailing men of Thugville on the other.

"For anybody who doesn't already know," Anarkey pronounced, "this town is under new management." He paused, then stepped toward Tuffy. "This wicked little pug has been fixing the game against you all from the beginning."

Tuffy tried to act outraged by this slander, but he didn't have the strength.

"You work to fill his pockets, and everything you need, he sells you. Well, no more. You work with us, you get a fair piece. If you don't want to work with us, no hard feelings. That's the way it's gonna be." Anarkey stared long at Tuffy. "I understand it's what people do."

The hogs immediately busied themselves around the cluttered sorting floor. They sifted through the inventory, assigning items to the best use of their new constituents, handing out staples and valuables to those who'd earned them. They answered every question about how things would change and how they wouldn't.

Crock limped gingerly toward the group, bringing Artie to an alarmed fighting stance. Crock lowered his posture with his hands up, and they talked at a safe distance. Crock said he'd never been cracked so hard and expressed his admiration and respect. He explained his life alone in the pipes under the city, and then described his life with Tuffy to the best of his ability.

The hogs stopped to listen with great sympathy until it was just Artie and Crock sitting together among stories of trying to fit in and feeling out of place. Artie told him about Pugville, and his mom and adoptive family. They laughed over the story of how the mules had fruit too sour to eat, how absurd it was that you couldn't enjoy food.

They soon joined Buster to find Tuffy's belongings and move them out to the street. Buster got brought into the conversation about being different, and the three became fast friends. They brainstormed about the most insensitive way of telling Tuffy to see Anarkey if he wanted a new place to live. They laughed so hard they had to rest several times.

Bertrand looked everywhere for Sarah. She'd disappeared in the fighting, and he couldn't think of where he'd seen her last. He scanned the house and shouted in different directions around the yard. She was gone. Bertrand sank to the ground in worry, his head in his hands, imagining the worst.

An old sea turtle, the very image of Bertrand himself, appeared at his shoulder with a soft tap. They gazed deeply into one another's eyes.

Bertrand shook his head and blinked fast, trying to clear his vision. He knew those eyes, but he'd never seen this creature before. He felt a comfortable presence, and his belly rumbled with butterflies. "Is it even possible?" he asked quietly.

"You know it is."

"But how? Why?" Bertrand just kept staring deeply into her eyes.

"You are a drifter, my friend. You don't put down roots. Your mission is to walk the earth seeking knowledge and helping others. I am the same."

Then came a familiar popping sound as the kindly turtle transformed into Sarah. She clacked her bear nails across his back as Bertrand welled up with tears of happiness.

"I had to know it was real before I told you," she said. "I had to know we were in love."

CHAPTER EIGHTEEN

Home

Bones and Earl were examining the Pugville floats with Jack and Cookie. In his own wonderful way of expressing gratitude to have the dogs back home and safe, Earl made a hundred snide remarks at the expense of the new craft and the old craftsmen.

As they loaded the boats for home, Moose excitedly showed Molly the controls and elucidated about wind and sails. He let her know that sailing was a thing he could easily teach her, him being expertly experienced.

Molly took it all in and immediately insisted the three children sail their own boat back home. They were grown now, in her opinion, and her brothers were men of the world.

Snuffy agreed wholeheartedly, over Tinkerbelle's stern objections. Snuffy then shot a look of terror at Sheriff Buck, who quietly promised to stay near the children, just in case.

Buster brought Clete and Clay along to help with their new friend Crock. Buster and Crock were still giggling over the meanest things they could think to say to Tuffy as they lifted items onto the boats.

Bertrand whispered to Snuffy his plan to swim the long way home with Sarah. Snuffy teased the old man for wanting to disappear with his girl, and Tinkerbelle shushed him. She gave them both a big kiss and wished them love.

Tuffy also stared over the beach, apart from the group, trying his best to reclaim a bit of his dignity. He casually suggested that he might visit Pugville one day, being that he owned a boat and had a bit of time on his hands.

Snuffy sneered at the selfish pug. "Well, I guess you can't pick your family."

"It's a free country," Tinkerbelle offered. "But please don't hurry."

"I might need a place to stay," Tuffy said, fishing for sympathy. "I'm not sure I'm entirely welcome here anymore."

"You can stay here as long as you want," Anarkey piped in. "Just stay out of my way."

Anarkey and Artemis walked down the beach a little together. They stood a long time in uncomfortable silence, casting their eyes across the water.

Anarkey finally found the words to tell his son. "You're a good and decent kid. And these are good and decent folks. It's best you go with them."

Artie was slightly shocked, although a little relieved. "But you're my real dad," he protested. "Shouldn't I stay here with you?"

"We'll never be far apart, now that we've found one another," Anarkey said. "You have a family that loves you. I'll always be your dad, just like Mercy will always be your ma. But you have a life over there."

Artemis cast his gaze to the ground.

"You're a remarkable boy," Anarkey continued. "Your mother would be proud of you."

Artemis teared up at the thought of the mother he didn't even remember. The things Bertrand said so long ago about his momma leaving him to the others rang in his head.

The two hogs embraced muzzle to muzzle, remaining close for a long time.

Anarkey finally broke the silence and looked his boy square in the eyes. "Go. Be a big brother and a good son. Thugville ain't no place for a pug like you."

The family boarded the boats and shoved off from the shore. Each boat caught a fair wind and blew steadily across the divide, appearing to shrink into the distant water.

Crock and Buster made their way back toward the compound, good friends beginning a new day in the neighborhood. Anarkey couldn't watch the boats any longer and followed closely behind.

Tuffy remained fixed on the shore, alone and damaged, nowhere to go.

THUGVILLE
UNKNOWN!

Thank you for enjoying The Pugville Chronicles.

To write a review, see bonus content, illustrations, and upcoming volumes please visit us at:
PugvilleChronicles.com
Facebook.com/pugvillechronicles
instagram.com/pugvillechronicles

Coming Soon:

The Pugville Chronicles

Volume Two:The Prequel

ABOUT THE AUTHORS

Kevin E. Thompson is a businessman, family man, and pug poppa emeritus from Southern California. Kevin developed the story of Pugville and the adventure of its creation over a lifetime of intense briefings from his loving pugs Rufio, Tinkerbelle, their parents and siblings. We have Kevin to thank for translating this history from the original pug. Kevin and his family make their home in the old neighborhood where our story begins, just down the block from the old jungle.

It is a cherished ambition for Kevin to bring these stories to the printed page, and his expertise as executive, mentor, and producer has given life to The Pugville Chronicles in a series of volumes, the first of which is proudly enclosed herein. Further volumes, including a prequel, are already in production. These chronicles presented as motion pictures cannot be far behind. Kevin and his family are tireless supporters of children's causes, and he hopes The Pugville Chronicles will be a source of inspiration, education, and practical application for years to come.

Michael Dean Jacobs is an actor and comedian from Southern California. He has been seen in movies, TV, nightclubs, and regional theatre since the late 20th century. Michael began his writing career when skits were popular on television, and when television was furniture with antennae.

This is Michael's first novel, crafted from the many stories related to him by Mr. Thompson. His canine experience is limited to dogs with pronounced noses, still he finds spiritual connection with all pedigrees, talking or otherwise. Michael currently resides in one large room with a typewriter somewhere in the hills beyond Las Vegas.

Made in the USA
Middletown, DE
27 May 2019